PRAISE FOR
The Autobiography of Vivian

"The funniest fictional heroine since Bridget Jones."
—*Teen People*

"The book is fodder for any woman who has dreams of living big despite humble beginnings."
—*USA Today*

"Vivian's autobiography reads like a conversation over coffee with a long lost friend. It is fun and sassy . . . and perfect for a sunny day at the beach or a rainy day on the couch."
—*Booklist*

"Vivian Livingston isn't a supermodel—she's a role model. . . . Vivian symbolizes the triumph of imperfection over perfection, for all women struggling with average bodies and often-problematic relationships, roommates, relatives, careers, co-workers, complexions, and menstrual cramps."
—*San Jose Mercury News*

"If you're looking for a light-hearted, humorous book to dive into as you wade out the rest of summer, this novel screams your name. . . . You will not be disappointed."
—*Las Vegas Mercury*

By Vivian Livingston and Sherrie Krantz
The Autobiography of Vivian

Vivian lives

by Vivian Livingston

AS TOLD TO SHERRIE KRANTZ

BALLANTINE BOOKS • NEW YORK

A Ballantine Book
Published by The Random House Publishing Group
Copyright © 2003 by Forever After, Inc.

www.ballantinebooks.com

Library of Congress Control Number: 2003094401

ISBN 0-345-45355-7

Cover illustration by Forever After, Inc.

Book design by Susan Turner

Manufactured in the United States of America

First Edition: August 2003

10 9 8 7 6 5 4 3 2 1

To the nameless, faceless individual responsible for a quote that I refer to often. One that I'm sure I read off a mug, magnet, or greeting card.

"TOUGH PEOPLE LAST, TOUGH TIMES DON'T."

So, to whoever you are, wherever you are, this one's for you. . . .

Acknowledgments

To my family for loving and supporting me. To Nikki & Stella, my sweet companions, who make sleeping alone a good thing. (De-de-de-de-de-de-de-de.) To the gutsy visionaries for the "pinch me" opportunities they've provided and the anecdotes they've shared. To Allison Dickens, my editor, who rocks and was also cool enough to extend my deadline. To my girls . . . for being in my life, inspiring and assuring me all the while. To J-Lo for being curvy. To Madonna for being ballsy. To Barry for being B-a-r-r-y. And finally, to every dickhead that I've had the displeasure of knowing, giving me enough lemons to make lemonade—pitchers of it.

Thank you.

prologue

There's something about happy endings that makes me feel like everything's possible. Even for a fleeting moment. Do you know what I mean? Suddenly I'm optimistic, adventurous, determined, confident . . . all things good. The future looks bright and I'm part of it. And I make a promise to myself to remember that feeling and live it when deemed necessary.

If you're wondering, YES, I'm part of that small majority—that group of gals who look in the mirror and see the negative before the positive. Overly sensitive, slightly neurotic. Yes it's true. My self-esteem plays me like a seesaw. I need that soundtrack, a cocktail, hell, the immediate-gratification impulse purchase to kick the week, the weekend, the evening off right. Pretty pathetic all things considered: the therapy, the achievements, the better-than-average job. But if you're looking for a rosy tale filled with bogus antidotes and naive untruths, you should probably set this novel down and head back to the chick lit table.

'Cause my story is real.

My ambition to fix what's broken, my fear of looking back with regret, the way I jones for first-kiss intensity every time around, and this relentless inner tic that feels as though it is deserving of anything that this once-in-a-lifetime life has to offer seems to always land me right smack in the thick of it. So far anyway.

My silent dreams and smallish wishes follow me around like puppy dogs. They constantly propel me to take chances. They make me believe in myself even if the odds are against me. And, suddenly, I become "that girl," the chick who throws one back and walks up to "that guy"—the one, of course, I think is out of my league. Likely, the same guy you chose not to make eye contact with 'cause you probably don't give yourself enough credit and instead make a buzzy beeline over to the coat check, wondering *what-if* during your cab ride home. I become the rookie in the conference room who every once in a while offers up an opinion while simultaneously receiving glares that could light a match from the venomous veterans who have learned to be agreeable. I don those threads even though they don't fit me quite the same way they do the sticks in the ads. I believe. I savor. I imagine. When I get a *Why?* I inevitably ask, *Why not?* And if I get a *no*—well, I'll bet you can guess what that does to me.

Now, now—before you get all cranky and think me arrogant and unrelatable, let me say this: Nine times out of ten my instincts are disastrous, the outcome becomes a bad joke, and the subtle confidence you're picking up on is undoubtedly underwritten with sweaty palms, a dry mouth, and a heart beating so boldly you'd think I had my own personal base turned up way too high.

But alas, what kind of person, friend, tenant to myself would I be if I quietly let my gluttonous gut go unheard? Seriously, if I can't sit through my own movie and leave the theater thinking,

"Yes! I really did live my life," well then a full refund is in order! And therein lies the problem. Doubtful any of us get a "refund" when our own credits start a rollin'. So I say this: Go for it. I did. I am. And I promise, I will. "Mistakes" or not, it's worth it. (Caution: I'm not suggesting we go leaping off small buildings in a single bound. Reckless is hardly the goal. Living big means something different to each of us.)

If nothing else, I know this to be true: Through the thick and thin of it all, it is with every harmless personal dare that I have found my greatest happiness.

Okay, so what are you waiting for? Pick me up, bring me to the checkout counter, and give me that personal attention I crave. I'm very low-maintenance actually. I love night-lights, don't get carsick, will eat anything, am fiercely independent, and am cool with a little downtime. But I do have one small request. When you're through with me and if you don't pass me on to your friend, cousin, or coworker: How 'bout resting me between that Brad Pitt unauthorized biography and Bruce Weber's most recent photography book?

What? It's all good. ☺

Cheers to you,

VIVIAN

oNe

Then:

I just have this feeling. I've been trying to lose it all evening but its persistence is weighing on me. It's Saturday night and I've been at the library, trying to dissect a thirty-second stint of a Hitchcock flick and write a twenty-page paper on it for this class I'm taking, *Film Theory*. My professor is an attractive woman, kind of delicate in a petite way, in her early forties, who wears mostly black, a few hints of white every now and again, and a constant red lipstick. Sometimes I notice the color bleeding beyond its normal expectations, filling in the lines and cracks that extend past the natural arcs and curves of her mouth and into the age of her tanned skin. She has green eyes and blunted ashy blond hair. She colors it. Or at least someone colors it for her. I can tell that she's got naturally dark hair under there and that fascinates me. Such the extreme. A college professor who credits vanity as a concern. She's very "New York" looking, maybe its because she lives there. She commutes in order to teach *Film Theory* to the likes of me in Pennsylvania. I find her unique. And I find her to be way more interesting than the twenty-page paper that I'm supposed to be writing—but it's not due actually for another few weeks so it's okay.

I'm driving, home I guess, in my car, an eight-year-old black, stick-shift two-door Mazda something-or-other. The ultimate hand-me-down, where my two older brothers surely made memories that I'm relieved they haven't shared. The ashtray is filled with change and rubber bands I use to tie back my hair. Or rubber bands my friends use to tie back their hair. Or rubber bands that their friends use to tie back their hair. There are a few unpaid parking tickets in my glove compartment and even more cracked CD cases—no CDs; they're probably in here somewhere. The plastic attachable coffee tray is cradling the coffee I picked up this morning on my way to the library. I only took a few sips. It was really hot. I take my coffee light and sweet. Now at the surface all I can see is white and a few crinkles of tan. I should probably dump that.

So I still have this feeling. Which is unusual because I don't usually feel much of anything. I mean I feel hot and cold, I feel that delayed rush of pain when I walk into the corner of something and stub my toe, but that's pretty much it. I feel angry and scared and sad most of the time, but I've grown so used to it that it just doesn't feel much like anything anymore. That's why this is such a strange night. 'Cause I have this feeling.

I feel like I want to rip my seat belt off. It's not like there's a seat belt law but one of the only automatic things about my eight-year-old hand-me-down Mazda is the seat belt. It zips around, passes right in front of my face, the minute I turn the key in the ignition. It feels confining suddenly now that I'm on the road, but if I try to rip it off I'm sure I'll get into an accident. So instead I roll down my window. All the way, going really fast, on a cold autumn evening on a Pennsylvania side street.

The wind fills my car and it doesn't make me cold. It makes

me certain. Certain of this something. So for all the time that I could count on just feeling cold, well now I feel only this feeling that tells me something's wrong. And of course I know that every-thing is wrong. But now something in my everything is wrong.

Instead of going home like I'm supposed to, I drive past my street and make a left on Mark's. No one is around really. The leaves on the oak trees are missing, too, and their wickery wiry branches have turned them into skeletons.

I live in a college town. A few stragglers are out walking their dogs; I can see them coming through the trees. It's Saturday night, so random weather-coated cars piled high with friends are picking someone up or dropping someone off. I don't have my watch anymore but I bet it's around eleven. And as I get closer and closer to his place I can feel my heart beating. It isn't beating fast. It's beating loud. And I'm careful to shut my lights off a few houses shy of his.

Everything looks normal. The house is dark. Mark and his roommate, Fred, are always out drinking by eight. It's a big house for just two guys. Mark lives on the ground floor. So I just sit there. In my car, in the dark, hoping that whatever it is that's drawing me to his house will subside now that I'm here. But it's just getting worse.

I have to go inside. If I don't, I know this dread will combust. Like an ache that has been simmering. Somewhat like fear but more like truth. I don't have a key anymore. (I lost it on purpose, in front of him, so he'd believe me.) But I figure he probably left something open. I know how he hates to carry much of any-thing. Afraid he'll lose his keys, I guess. We worked it out that I'd be at the library and go to bed early tonight. And that I'd sleep at my place 'cause he'd be coming home late and didn't want to wake me.

It's been a few minutes and I just have to go in. The fear, the truth, is getting really loud and is beginning to hurt. I hug myself cozy in my navy bubble jacket. It's warm and down-filled. It gives me a slight comfort as I walk up the driveway and around the back to the sliding glass doors in the kitchen. It's so quiet. I can hear the gravel and then the grass beneath my shoes. Reminds me of Rice Krispies in the morning.

The door is unlocked. I am right. I like that I am right. The house is so still and quiet and dark. I leave the door open a bit behind me. His neighbor, a quiet guy, has his TV on upstairs, and that bit of light is just enough to allow me to see where I'm going. My insides are amplified. I'm not sure what I'll find, if anything at all. I'm not sure about what I want to find, if anything at all. I just know something is wrong and that something bad might or might not happen, but I feel like I don't have a choice. I have to be here. I have to see it or not see it. My gut is emerging from the inside out and is in complete control.

Mark's brown leather bomber jacket that I gave him for Christmas last year is hanging over one of the mismatched chairs in his kitchen. He looks so handsome in that jacket. I put my hand on the collar. It's cold. He's here. In the house. I grab it and take it with me as I walk down the hallway toward his room.

I'm getting really thirsty and really sweaty. My throat begins to stick together and for a second I can't find any air. My eyelids feel very heavy and each time I blink it feels as though weights are being added. My heart is screaming slowly. I'm aware of my body, of my mind, and of what I'm doing and where I'm travel-ing at this very moment. I'm my own witness. I stretch my right arm out in front of me and hold his cold jacket to my heart with my left. I find the door and rest my fingertips on its rough wood surface. I can feel the dip and the splintering and the small tears in the surface, remembering quickly how they arrived there the week or month before. I hear nothing. My brain tells my fingers to apply a small bit of pressure to the door while I just watch. My body leans forward and my wide eyes peer in. I see nothing. I reach for the light and flick it on. Still nothing.

I'm relived and I'm disappointed and I'm tired. Show's over. Day's over. I decide to crash.

I grab his sweats that are hanging from the top corner of his closet door and put them on. I still love wearing his sweats. They are so big and sloppy and worn all the way through. They make me feel sweet. I can imagine him being happy to see me sleeping in his bed when he gets home. I switch off the light and bundle myself under his covers and backtrack to my suspicions. "Neah" I think to myself.

It's still so quiet. And in a house this big it's scary. I reach for the remote on the end table and turn on his television. The noise is immediate and shocking and I scurry to find MUTE. And in the next second I hear a thump from above and then a scuffle and then a thump and before I can think I bolt out of bed, down the hallway, up the stairs, and down another hallway. I'm taken aback by the slamming and then a lock to Fred's bedroom door.

Without thought:

I shout, "Hello?"

Nothing.

"Hello?"

Nothing.

"Fred?"

Nothing.

I start pounding on the door.

Nothing.

Pounding.

Nothing.

Again I watch as I pound and kick the door. I listen as I shout, fearlessly, "Open the door Mark . . . Open it NOW!!!"

Nothing.

"I'm not going to move, I will never leave this door," I say. "So open it . . . NOW!" I cry. I stand there with my back to the wall, whimpering, exhaustion three years in the making, purging itself. I relinquish my strength and slide down with my legs outstretched and then finally my chin to my chest, my hands over my eyes.

I hear whispers and more movement but I don't get up until I hear slow heavy footsteps coming toward me. Nearly transfixed, I watch the knob of the door make a careful semicircle and by the time I look up, there is Mark filling the doorway in boxers and an awkward smile from ear to ear.

"What are you doing here, Vivi? Are you crazy?" he says. He is so big and so tall and so wide that there is no view behind him. But I know someone is there. I know this because he is nervous and polite. Polite for him. Had he been alone or among friends he would have easily skipped the small talk and gotten down to it.

I just look into his eyes. Small in comparison to mine. My shoulders hunched over. My head heavy on my neck, tilting back. His big droopy sweatpants hang on only by the bony bones of my hips. He just smiles and laughs and shakes his head from side to side. It is always in this, the middle, where I try to break through and summon the girl I was when we first met and come to my senses. And I find her all right, but instead of leaving, fast and furious, she rages, forgets her size, forgets his strength, and allows the misery, anguish, and desperation to anchor her.

It's in this split second that I hear "her"—a new voice but always the same. And quickly, as he looks behind him, I seize the moment to rush under his arm and through the door and there she is, covered only by the covers. With pretty dark straight black hair, tanned skin, and an expressionless expression.

I say nothing and hear yelling, words that don't sound like

much of anything, and then my head bangs quickly against the old wood floor and I'm out and it's peaceful.

The slamming of a door wakes me. It wakes me seconds before a hard kick to my side startles me. I don't get up quickly enough for him and so he lifts me, abruptly, with his two hands and two thumbs carving through each of my underarms. As I open my eyes I see him move away from me. Away from me as I am slammed into the wall I don't even realize is behind me. Then I am coming toward him and then rushed back again and again back into the wall. Over and over. There's yelling that I still can't make out.

He makes me stand up straight with my back against the wall, and he gets angrier and angrier with me. I don't have enough energy to hold myself up and as I begin to fall he grabs my long hair to make sure that I stay still. But I can feel the tiny hairs breaking from their roots and I know he can, too. So he lets me loose and I again fall to the floor.

I can feel the moist warm mist of his saliva hit my face and roll down my chin. It gets in my eye and in my mouth. He gets exasperated because I still have no fighting words for him and yet I can still look at him as he screams and shouts. I lie there fighting not to close my eyes; I'm afraid this time that they will never open. Look at him. Look at him. That's all that I can think about.

There is silence and he is gone. My brain tells my arms to help me up but they don't listen. My brain tells my head to move from side to side but it doesn't listen. And then there's water. Icy cold prickly water all over. I see Mark looking scared. Waiting for me to react. And I do. It's cold. And I love it. I love the water. I am thankful for it. And I must be smiling. For a time I haven't disappeared. Mark then lifts me back up, and carries me down the stairs and places me in his bed. He puts the television on, tucks me in. I feel cold. Then I feel freezing. My top is soaked.

I sleep a heavy sleep, waking up forgetful of the night before until I try to move. I cock my head to the side and see Mark. He is white and without sleep. His deep green eyes bloodshot and swollen.

"I'm so sorry, Vivi."

I say nothing.

He lays his head on my chest and weeps but I am still really out of it. I'm too roughed up to be angry just yet. I'm too worn out for a discussion. Which is usually how it goes.

"I panicked last night. I thought for sure you would leave me. I lost control and look what I did to you. I love you. It's because I love you, Vivi. Please forgive me. Don't leave me. I'm so sorry."

two

Now:

With fingerless black cashmere gloves I wrapped my hands around a much-needed cardboard cup of piping hot watered-down deli hot chocolate. I took a sip anyway, knowing it would scald the tip of my tongue, but the fine fresh scent of cocoa was all too alluring. And besides, it was New York's first real autumn evening and—having misplaced my cash card yet again—I knew I'd need some sort of insulation as I made the twenty-something-block trek, which would have otherwise been a convenient cab ride, to Man-Ray, the latest and greatest new restaurant where I was meeting my gregarious group of girlfriends for chow.

I took my time even though I didn't have much and was thankful that my heels weren't that high, nor my jeans so tight that I couldn't enjoy the walk. I could make my stroll into something more. A trip down memory lane. (Knowing the shortcuts.) I laughed silently, having spotted my dusty rose smooch stain on the cup's plastic top. So girly, I thought. The streets were sloppy with lights, cameras ($89.99—not bad), and plenty of action. Slammed with overachievers and theatergoers. Out-of-towners upsetting the natives as they break every unwritten rule. Again, I felt pleased knowing I had one up on them all: I didn't fit in either category and could see it all coming a mile away. The best of both worlds.

From one corner to the next, giant glass boxes surrounded stores, dollar shops, eateries, and theaters—as cluttered as an out-of-the-wrapper suburban cul-de-sac. No space, breathing room, rhyme, or reason. But there was a busy gritty charm to it all. And then I thought of Sophie, my lifelong best friend, and yet another (new) reason why she loved our second city so much: I was walking down a never-ending full-length wall-to-wall mirror. Oops, and I'd better fix my scarf.

I'd been waiting on this Thursday night all week. The first few months at the Web site had been much more than I'd bargained for, and getaways such as this were becoming too few and far between. And let me just say that unless you are a smaller-than-average finned creature you should likely think twice before signing a lifelong lease on a fishbowl.

It was also Sophie's one-week anniversary—with herself. Tonight marked seven days sans a cigarette (again) and I wanted to buy her some *stick-with-it* roses. But without a dime to my name, the thought was just going to have to count for something. I amused myself at a dingy bodega for a while, watching in amazement as a pint-sized employee spray-painted the flowers for sale along its perimeter. Yup. NYC is probably the only place where anticipatory young men and pairs of roommates will wait curbside for their surgically enhanced bouquet of color.

Moving right along, I picked up my pace. I was now running late. And it was getting rather chilly. Yum. Chili. (Mom makes a mean turkey chili.) Much like a great cardio tape, the traffic had been so tight that I had two young guns in a souped-up camouflage SUV to thank for the background music. Every little bit helped these lazy legs. The tunes got me thinking, too. Of a few out-of-control evenings, when I'd first moved here. Scamming my way into clubs, dancing for hours to the point where I was sure I'd wake up the next morning at least a half an inch shorter. Remembering Sophie in a barely there tank top, likewise lip syncing along to our favorite song, both thinking, *Pinch me* and *Are we really even here?* Although it had only been a couple of years it felt like a lifetime ago. Ahhhhhhh, memories.

It was as I was held up at the next street's corner that I saw a familiar face waiting, too, facing my direction and also obeying traffic. The face threw me back, way back, and briskly I staged a phony phone call, looking down and into my purse, hoping the face wouldn't see me back, trying just the same to ease the rush of memories. I speed dialed my own apartment and heard my own voice, one that now seemed completely foreign, and I hung up. I crossed the street in the nick of time and leaned against the closest storefront window in order to catch my breath.

I breathed a sigh of relief, trying to maintain my composure and sustain my mood. I reminded myself of where I was, where I was going, and whom I was about to see. I tried to find my music but couldn't and gathered it was long gone.

Jesus, I thought. *It's been nearly five years since Film Theory.*

I wondered if I'd always feel like I was in hiding. Like a lifelong member of the witness protection program. NYC was to be my sanctuary, starting over, starting fresh, and it was rare that my move to the city ever possessed a "run and hide" aspect to it. But suddenly, in the solitude of my own body, in the confines of my own mind, forgetting the new address, new job, new look, and new man, I was stricken with the past, with fear, with a realness so strong that it put a big fat kibosh on everything.

I stood there, trapped from the inside out. Feeling like a

weakling, dressed up like a champ. It was as if Mark stood before me, almost in my way. Trying to ruin my dinner and prevent me from seeing my friends. Concealing a threat with a smile. Ownership and control with a theoretical profound understanding of my wants and needs. "Who's fooling who?" I could hear him say.

A firey exchange between two cabdrivers got my attention and inadvertently removed Mark from my way. I jumped on the distraction and I thought about my life as it is today. Who I am now. Not Film Theory, not a dried-up professor, not a beat-up girlfriend.

It took a concerted effort to inch my way out from the storefront corner and continue my walk downtown. Getting my groove back is a drill I've been practicing for years. My own mind game that I've come to accept rather than question. It's as though I've maxed out on repression. There's no more room. So when feelings and memories hit the forefront, I allow them their due. But with every fiber, every bit of energy, I do what it takes to move forward and step back into my shoes—the ones that fit.

Seeing my professor brought me right back, and yes, it was more than a buzz kill. But surrendering to a memory, a flashback, is not me anymore. Yes, my night was affected by it and dinner was at best okay. But, I went. I went with a smile that early on felt forced but before long, felt comfortable.

It's all about getting back in my saddle these days.

three

So there's the matter of "the Web site," www.vivianlives.com. The online destination where the life and times of a twenty-something New Yorker *(moi)* are the gotcha gimmick of a community-based, service-oriented, chock-full-o'-eye-candy home away from home. The definitive "girls rule" Web site of its time, if you will. (And, if you ask me!)

After that first meeting with the Forever After, Inc., team (they're the ones backing the site), when I'd told my nearest and dearest that I was quitting my job at VH1 to be the featured player of a start-up dot.com, all who were closest to me didn't think it was the greatest idea. The Web site—yeah, sure, cool concept, but the *moi* part? No! (Not including, of course, Sophie and co.—they were beyond thrilled. Thought it was the best idea since sliced bread and the opportunity of a lifetime for me.) My parents, who are easily the most low-profile private people on the planet, made up their minds in an instant. Immediately they thought of all the freak shows out there in the U-S-of-A who would have quick-draw access to my whereabouts. Try this on for size: My mother gave me a whistle on a neon string as my going-away present when I first left Pennsylvania for the Big Apple, so you do the math. My brother Joseph thought about every pervert walking the planet and the grief he'd get from his friends. My boyfriend, Jack, well, he pretty much shared the sentiment.

Sophie, on the other hand, had thought of the access—the parties, the premieres, the clothes, the recognition—and she practically dragged me to the first real semisealed "audition." (Semisealed 'cause although I was the front-runner there were still two other girls under consideration.) Looking back, it was very much like the ritualistic drama Omelet, my puppy, gives me on the way to the groomer. I feel like a borderline Mommy-Dearest, the way I have to drag him as he desperately plants all four paws into the charcoal pavement, fighting all the way. Sophie was pulling on my leash the same way I pull on Omelet's, telling me I would love it once I got there. It's not like I was exactly against the opportunity at hand. Being the Web's first It girl did kinda have a nice ring to it, but I was petrified, going in, meeting all the bigwigs, hoping that I'd measure up. Sophie, though, would have none of it.

"Do it for me," she'd insist as I'd look at her with an *I-don't-know* seasick-ish grin. Hell, could I blame her? The upside was really really up, ya know? And honestly, before there was enough time to even ponder that very question, it was easy to see, eye to eye, that had I chickened out, she'd wonder who it was she was looking at. Up until this point, *Just Do It* had been my tagline—and we were all convinced Nike had stolen it from me!

Anyway, obviously, I got the gig (the name of the site kinda gives it away: www.vivianlives.com). Deep breathe here. And I felt like a bit of a lab rat in the beginning. I didn't necessarily get why I was their choice. In a city with so many interesting, beautiful, talented, women/girls who are made for the pace and the pressures, girls who have accomplished so much, who are friends with "this one" and "that one," who dated or were dating Mr. So-and-so, who were comfortable in front of a camera—I understandably was overcome by insecurity and self-doubt. The *why-me* syndrome in full effect. And of course, I had no choice but to suffocate every last bit of it.

Every day was an exercise in futility. "They like me for me," I'd sing (not aloud, of course, except when no one was looking). Not because I'm friends with Leonardo . . . Seriously, that was my theme song! Talk about Dr. Jekyll and Ms. Hyde. I was as insistent on embracing myself as I was neurotic that that same self was so so so not good enough.

But let's fast-forward, shall we? The only way I'd been able to keep my head on straight for the past three years since that audition won me a starring role on the World Wide Web, and not second-guess every single thing I say or do, is by pretending that the Web site does not exist at all. Allow me to explain: See, the site offers a window into my life. Literally. Through Webcams that have been renamed "Viv-cams" and virtual entry into my apartment. My journal writings and daily musings, "a day in the mind and life of . . . ," tie everything else on the site together. And the whole thing would be a huge house of cards if I let my nerves or the expectations of others stand in my way. So, I guess if nothing else, I brought strong will to the audition/table. That's got to be why they picked me.

But, if it's all right with you, I'd love it if we could just move ahead, knowing that all along, throughout the pages of this book, I've been moonlighting for nearly three years as the gatekeeper of a Web site.

That being said, I also had a normal "day job," and a pretty interesting one at that. I was the marketing manager at Forever After, Inc.

As I'm sure you're well aware, a successful Internet site needs a kick-ass marketing department. Because, hey, that's what it's all about. Marketing, in my humble opinion, is the basis on which all key elements of a business thrive. From traffic, to the all-important "cool factor," to advertising—aka "kwan." And because I had dabbled in public relations (a glam-o-fied version of marketing) during my tenure at VH1, I was made marketing manager, one of a team of six.

My position within the company actually helped balance me out, internally that is, because I knew that I brought something tangible to the table. Still not comfortable in my own camera-shy shoes, at least as marketing manager my experience and contacts in the music world and in production (special events, promotion) were real and obvious.

My job description was a little fuzzy at first. I was basically a glorified assistant until everyone got settled in and comfortable. And that, looking back, didn't take all that long. I had my own small office, a converted closet to be honest, but an office just the same. And for those of you with a similar cubicle-heavy history, I'm sure you get exactly where I'm coming from. I felt like CEO and then some!

My "teammates," as I was brainwashed to call them, were fantastic. We all got on brilliantly. All but one ('cause there's always one right) and, of course, the "one" for me was my boss. Stan (executive VP, advertising and marketing). He "disliked" me and yet he was in the ironic position of having to like me, because not only did I work for him, but as the namesake of the Web site he also had to promote me, twenty-four seven.

See, I'm pretty sure that when Stan signed on for the position, he thought he'd have the chance to become best friends with a Hilton sister or something. I'm sure he envisioned "parislives.com." At the very least someone whom he felt warranted all the hype and visibility. Someone who was on a first-name basis with the salespeople at Barney's. A girl who'd show up on NYC's most eligible bachelorette list. Stan was all about "breaking in." Breaking in, that is, to the small supposedly enviable crowd that dominates the pages of most glossy magazines. His job at FAI (Forever After, Inc.) was going to be the ladder he so desperately needed. Fat chance. So yeah, imagine his dismay when he had to talk, think, breathe, basically coexist with the likes of me—a small-town girl, size eight (okay ten, but this is my story so there!), without a credit card or a trust fund to speak of.

Anyhoo, not everyone was like Stan. In fact, I think a lot of my peers were pleasantly surprised when they realized that they could teach me a thing or two. Take May, for instance. Stan's right hand. (Poor thing.) She's awesome. Direct, to the point, funny, and shared my enthusiasm for all leading men. We got on grand! (One of my best pals today actually.) May had gone to NYU to study film and then when everyone and their mother became fascinated by the Internet, the idea of being a struggling filmmaker got much less attractive. She graduated early and charmed her way into Stan's employ. For me May is the ultimate girlfriend. Like when you need that honest opinion and you're not afraid to hear it, May's the one. Hint: Don't ever ask her if the dress you're already wearing to that party is flattering. When you're skirting around an issue and all your other friends are telling you what you already know or what they think you want to hear!—May's your girl. And I think in a strange way I was "that girl" for her, too.

Moving on, just below Stan was Drew. Not exactly my boss, but for a while there he definitely thought he was. Luckily it was a power struggle filled with just enough sexual tension that I let it slide. He was cute. Very very cute. In a Foo-Fighter-ish way. And let me just add, Drew was Mr. Contemplated Casual. You just knew he spent loads of time and loads of money to make it look like he didn't. Perfectly touseled brown hair. Denim jeans weathered to perfection. Always just loose enough that he'd have to don that Kid Rock clan belt. And that great black sweater. So soft that you knew it was cashmere. Retro-looking, retro-fitting kicks—sneakers he probably found on eBay. Ones you hadn't seen in forever. Unmarked, unscathed, carefully laced. And then there was his choice of cologne, excuse me, cucumber oil, dabbed in all the right places. P-L-E-A-S-E! The effort!!! I was betting his real name was An-drew and he still got mad at his mom if she slipped! He had an interesting job: VP, marketing. Creating programs for advertisers above and beyond "the banner." So if advertiser X spent a lot of money with FAI, Drew had to dance. A little bit like what I'd done at VH1. Cross-marketing and merchandising. Executing ideas that involved our Web site but then went one step farther: sweepstakes, tours, in-store events, etc. He also made sure the invites, guest lists, charity, etc., were all very "Vivian." (Sounds funny, right?) He lived with his then girlfriend—a sittings editor at a top fashion mag whose name I never knew. (As described to me by Sophie, a sittings editor is someone who is always actually on the shoot. Making sure all the players from photographers, to stylists, groomers, etc. are shooting the pictures in the way the magazine intended. Obscure, sleek, product-driven, sexy, what have you.) I just called her "But." Because that's how he always described her:

"She's great, but . . ."

"We've been living together for two years, but . . ."

"My parents really like her, but . . ."

Pathetic.

Anyway, "An-Drew" and I gave each other enough hell that work, when he was around, felt a lot more like recess.

Sheryl dominated the PR arm of our department. Diva! Came right out of the fashion world. And unlike Drew, if you couldn't identify who made what on her person, she was devastated. Even casual Friday was a label-whore moment. Dior T-shirt, skintight and cropped of course, low low low Seven jeans, straighter-than-straight brown hair, and never ever anything less than two-inch heels. (Casual shoes to Sheryl were suede.) Bottom line: Flips-flops were only for the privacy of your own home. She was the Jewish Donatella Versace, Long Island accent and all. But you had to love her. Easily the hardest-working girl in the building. (Have you seen our press coverage? I rest my case.) Sheryl had black-and-white pictures of her and her friends, her and her dogs, her and her parents, her finishing the marathon, her making a funny face at a camera, her with celebrity X, musician Y, athlete Z everywhere. Her office was her own homage to herself, carefully canvased along every wall. Noteworthy: She had a Precor in there as well. Said her best ideas came when she could feel the burn—scary!

And then there was Marni, in the unenviable position of working for two and a half people: Drew, Sheryl, and me (sort of). New to New York City. Her stepmother had relocated here and, with no life plan after college she followed suit, after obtaining her diploma. She was shyer than shy and shyer than me. With huge huge huge boobs that innocently started every meeting, blond hair, giant brown eyes with lashes so long and luscious that you thought they were false. At five-foot-two, she was sweet and competent and earnest, but it was also easy to see what Stan may have seen in Marni when he hired her. She had a cat, Siamese, named Shakespeare, and a boyfriend named Steven who was still getting his last few credits back in Alabama. They were to be engaged in the coming months and it was over many a Happy Meal that I tried to get to the bottom of her blatant content. The fact that she "just knew" that Steven was "it" was a completely foreign concept to me. "Rest of your life" was something that I had a lot of trouble getting my head around. Marni would smile whenever we talked about Steven. In fact it was only when we talked about Steven or Shakespeare that her brown eyes ever lit up.

So there you have it—the dream team: Stan, Drew, Marni, Sheryl, May, and little old me. My virtual and slightly dysfunctional family. Responsible, easily, for my impending nervous breakdown, taxed friendships, and absolutely one or two of my breakups with Jack. God, I wish I could say that I was kidding.

four

It was another fine fresh morning but my buzz was killed the minute I saw the ELEVATOR OUT OF SERVICE sign on, of course, every elevator in the lobby of my office building. (That'll be nine floors, ladies—first thing in the morning, in sky-high patent-leather mary janes with my coffee, the paper, and a heavy black messenger bag filled with my stuff from last night!)

As I made my way up the stairs, I quickly attempted a Jedi mind trick. I had my coffee to contend with: too expensive to leave behind, nearly too hot to hold, and so brown that it'd better not spill on my crisp white fresh-from-the-cleaners button-down blouse. My distraction? The boyfriend—Jack.

I had spent the night before at his place. He had this dark cozy extra-large raw space in Dumbo, one of the few yet-to-be-developed sections of Brooklyn. It doubled as his studio, which gave it a charm and an honesty that touched me. It reminded me of a log cabin jammed and hidden in what still felt like "Gotham" to a newbie like me. With views of the Manhattan skyline and the Brooklyn Bridge, and a collection of vintage vinyl jazz records, when I stayed there we usually wound up "staying in." Some wine, that view, and those records—it got me every time!

We'd been together for a while. We were at that "midmark" where the sex, when we had it, was good and the conversation, again, when we had it, was meaningful. Nothing was sugar-coated, bodily functions were "natural," and we never had to ask the other what to bring home from the deli on a late-night run. It was the relationship I'd always dreamed of having, but alas, the realities didn't come with a warning label:

> **WARNING:** *First healthy relationship with mature, responsible guy your parents approve of and your friends love may cause drowsiness, headaches, anxiety, disinterest, nausea, and/or dry mouth. You may wish to consult your physician if you have been craving an argument, resenting said gentleman, harboring feelings of guilt, or questioning self-worth.*

You know how they say that the best man for you is your opposite 'cause he'll complement you? Rub off on you? Expand your horizons even? Well, I thought that was all rubbish.

JACK
Healthy
Neat
Rational
Responsible
Sweet
Artistic

*He cooked, too.

Notice my list of my own attributes is missing.

Now on floor three, I thought about this great guy. About the apartment I'd just left.

About the mountain bike that hung in his hallway. The mail and his keys and the small silver photo frames filled with family, friends, and one of me that rested on his entryway table. The squeaky old wood flooring. The single exposed brick wall that coated his palatial place and the dark gray velvet couches that inhabited it. The Sunday sports section bent and bruised. The set-less throw pillows. The old spare blanket. The other woman—his new fancy television. (TiVo and all.) His unhung art-work left on opposite sides of his fireplace. The hardworking can-dles, with cloudlike bubbles that cascaded over and onto his mahogany coffee table that he'd made himself the year be-fore.

Rugs, rugs, rugs.

His refrigerator. The magnets. The beer and soda and ener-gizer juices. The Tupperware filled with leftovers, extras, and for-laters. The freezer jammed with frozen cuts from the market and a few pints of you-know-what. Ice trays with no ice. The dishes done.

The white-on-white bathtub. The filmy shaving mirror suc-tioned to the tiled perimeter. The dull checkerboard floor. The worn navy towels, damp. The laundry bag filled with sweaty T-shirts earned from this event or another and the tattered denim jeans that always looked really good.

Schedules, calendars, ticket stubs, a few flyers, and a Po-laroid of us, all tacked up on the bulletin board mounted inches above his desk. On which sat his dad's old typewriter (Jack didn't own a computer), a charcoal portrait of his niece Tatum, the cordless phone with the nibbled antenna (Omelet had a "moment"), his answering machine, and week after week's worth of *Sports Illustrated*'s. A long cherry-red box that housed the tie he'd been meaning to return since Christmas and the photo I'd taken, the previous spring, of Jack, his brother, his brother-in-law, and his dad, arm over arm, all in uniform, New York City firefighters, as handsome and as real as they come.

"The Corner." His studio—naked, rusty, urban. Materials, tools, unfinished business.

His closet. Two suits. Jeans, jeans, jeans. Sweaters, sweatshirts, kicks, kicks, kicks. The flimsy narrow full-length fifteen-dollar mirror I insisted he get, screwed into the inside door. Smooch-stained at the top right corner—I planted it just for fun.

The low warm mushy king-sized bed. My side. His side. Covered in midnight-blue linens baked to perfection by the old radiator that lined the single but sizable window at the apartment's end. His trusty alarm clock—my nemesis—propped perfectly on one of his treasured books, *Lou Gehrig: The Luckiest Man on Earth*. The tiny plaid bed and ivory porcelain bowl for Omelet when he slept over, a very cozy arrangement. Tapes and tapes, records and records. This ball and that ball. Photo albums. Books, books, books. His underwear from last night.

It was crowded in a careful way. Chaos, easily, were it not for his structure. The only space was the space itself and the man of the house was a happy one.

That was Jack.

I surveyed Jack's place often. And tested myself when I wasn't there. An odd little habit that nagged as though it needed to be licked. I tried to believe that the more I knew it—the few dust bunnies in the corners, the five light switches, the frog-shaped water stain on the bathroom ceiling, the seven little scuffs that inhabited its four walls—it would come to feel familiar and not in an unfamiliar way.

I didn't think about the women who'd come before me. I never left a single article there. It was his place. His smell. His light. With not a bad memory to be found, and I was pretty sure that was what I was looking for.

Ninth floor. Finally.

five

Try to imagine . . . My coffee made it nine long flights, right? But then I turn my back (literally) for five quick seconds. Without a free hand, I opted to use my rear to push open the heavy steel door, and forces beyond my control kicked in and—bloop, drip, splat—the sudden force of movement jockeyed my coffee cup and my entire left nipple ended up brown. Apropos I guess.

To make matters worse, Drew was maybe two legs behind me, caught my little morning moment, and enjoyed the irony. He winked and stepped right past me—in and onto our floor. Not even so much as a *Wow. That sucks. Can I give you a hand?*

I couldn't stand him.

Well, that wasn't entirely true.

It was Monday and the office was a-flurry. Filled with psyched-up employees who'd convinced themselves that this was going to be "their" week. Likely, having consumed enough alcohol over the weekend to forget how sucky their previous Friday had been. The kitschy company kitchen, with its faux and finicky automatic cappu-, mocha-, and frappuccino maker, was as crowded as a small It bar during happy hour on a Thursday night. Ahhh, there they were. Yeah, "Hi," whatever . . . the cats in the expensive suits, trying to make small talk with the techies in the baggy vintage cords and colorful Converse kicks. Kids to the core who made more money than any of us, yet cursed the contrived conditions of their employ.

"Sorry V," Sheryl murmured, whizzing by me with her shellacked fake tan and a plastic Starbuck's coffee mug.

Marni was miserable. She saw her boyfriend off at La Guardia at seven A.M.

May had a smile on her face. "Hiiiiiiiiiiiiii." She'd just walked to work and in her healthier-than-thou masochistic way easily enjoyed the added nine-inch nail incline.

Before I could even get to my own hospice, shut the door, change my top, and find a smile, the streaky sunlight screamed from the conference room, and then there was the *join-us* gesture, à la Stan, that I'd been conditioned to dread. Corneas nearly nuked, I obliged. As if Monday morning sans an elevator weren't hard enough—let's have another micromanaged meaningless meeting to talk about the all-important advertising dollar and how we couldn't seem to find it under strobelike light. Light that made the guys sweat through the armpits of their dark blue broadcloth shirts and, likewise, made the girls regret that they'd skipped their Sunday waxing appointment.

I just love Mondays.

six

I barely thought I'd make it through that Monday. My coffee-soaked blouse (replaced with a loaner from May), a larger than normal cell phone bill that I hadn't been prepared for, an ardent call from my mom, the details of which I'll spare you, and then there's the daily Stanfactor. . . . That day it was his intolerable whining about the budget. I've nearly recovered. Nearly. All of that coupled with the fact that I had a very special evening planned with Jack. Six o'clock felt like it would never ever find me! But finally, Jack and I were seated next to each other, hand in hand, third row center at Radio City Music Hall, about to see David Gray—one of the few musicians we both really love. Nearly maxed out with anticipation, I'd been looking forward to this for weeks, and nights like this didn't come around too often. Rarely does Jack have much interest in the handful of invites I get each month. He's a low-profile guy, strong, even basic at times. He never lets his "stuff" get to him. It's as if he possesses an instinctual scale that keeps him balanced for those tortured angst-filled moments when the "artist" in him gets his better. Without a scale of my very own, I could only envy his.

He was excited. I could tell, and much to my surprise I embraced the sense of responsibility that had been lingering since we'd gotten here: The evening's entertainment was on me. I dug that it was because of my work that we were here tonight. My boss's boss had been unable to go, she gave the tickets to Stan, and, well, voilà! (Let's hear it for my "perks" . . . let's give my perks a ha-an-an-and. *Footloose*—c'mon!)

It was great 'cause neither of us had ever sat so close to a stage, not counting school plays. The only downside that I could spot was that Jack was too big for his chair. He's uncomfortable and trying to hide it, but his squishing and squashing gives him away. The denim of his favorite jeans, tight around his quads, damp from the wet weather. His knees nearly in his throat. Poor thing. My eyes followed his legs, traveled past his ankles, and spotted his gray New Balance kicks. I smiled inside. They reminded me of the day we first—well, really, the day we second met.

His well-worked frame was hidden behind a retro-looking navy-and-white Adidas warm-up jacket. It was zipped up almost all the way and I loved loved loved that only I knew there was a hole in the heather-gray T-shirt he was wearing underneath. I knew there was a hole where the washed-out tag used to be. Before he'd yanked it off one hot morning not a handful of months ago while we'd brunched outside along the Hudson River at a cute little eatery in Brooklyn. It was hot. Sticky hot. And he'd agreed to sit outside in the sun rather than inside where both the huge commercial air conditioner and the baseball game were on. He'd agreed to do this because he knew how much I enjoyed eating outside. (People-watching, puppies allowed, Jackie O shades, etc.)

Now, sitting beside him, I also loved knowing that Jack would probably sleep in that same gray T-shirt tonight. I loved knowing that he often tended to do that. "Dress for bed" as I liked to call it. Instead of thinking about what would be great for the evening ahead, like most people, my boyfriend considered what he'd most like to sleep in, before he got dressed to go out. (Don't even ask.)

"My boyfriend"—wow—I still wasn't used to it.

I was getting antsy. Jack could tell and squeezed my right hand in his left. His right arm, extended, was resting on his thigh. I could see the red-stringed Buddha bracelet I'd knotted around his wrist the past summer. I couldn't believe he was still wearing it. That hand. I loved when it gripped on to the back of my neck when we took slow walks home from the movies.

The lights in the theater dimmed slightly, signaling the start of the performance. I couldn't wait. We both couldn't wait. Jack cocked his head in my direction and smiled. I loved the way that single thick tooth, just a few down from the center, left, did a delicate Dracula-like thing when I caught his happiness. The way his full lips snuggled his teeth, tucked in, halfway. I loved that that mouth was mine. Yum.

The place went dark. And at a moment's notice, David Gray emerged and, behind him, three supersized extra-large video screens with black-and-white then color-washed montages of every pretty place you could imagine. "Sail Away" was his first song. My favorite.

The music started, I got settled in my seat—loving it. But slowly I began to feel isolated, almost sedated. A sweet sadness all my own. It was unexpected and gradually I was heavy with emotion, heavy with thought, I pulled my hand out from Jack's and I zoned out. Even with my eyes wide open, the world around me went dark. I couldn't see a thing. David's voice, his words, the earnestness of it all completely jibed with the melancholy of my mood. Beautiful pain if there was such a thing. He stroked his guitar sluggishly, and I could feel it in my bones. Like a deep-tissue massage, that in the wrong mind-set, can make you want to cry.

Fighting back tears, I felt Jack's cold fingertips as he delicately stroked my cheek, brushing back a crimped curl of my hair. There was a flash when I wanted to look his way to reassure him I guess, but I didn't and the moment disappeared into the music. And then I couldn't.

I feel Jack again. He placed his hand around the top of my thigh. His last two fingers fell over my curves. He wanted to con-nect. To touch. But it all felt inconsequential. My mind and heart are elsewhere.

As the song lingers on, I'm haunted by Mark. And my memo-ries, although vivid, seem distorted and confused. He's apolo-gizing, over and over again. It's like a fantasy and I'm too captivated to push him away. There is a sober second when I want to get back into the now. To think of Jack and not let my past take over another evening in the present. But I can't. The contents of me seem to be drifting away with the sound of every instrument, every lyric, every verse. Like I was floating over the ocean, an ocean of heartbreak. Oscillating along with the cur-rents, the atmosphere slowly pulls me farther and farther away from the land. Mark is with me and after a while there's peace, there's forgiveness, there's love, and we're together.

The latter part of this *delusion* was enough to shut it off. Con-fused, ashamed, disgusted, and most of all sad, I lean over to Jack, wrap both my arms around his one, squeezed then pushed my weight into my heels, allowing my lips to reach his cheek. I kiss him gently and then relax my body and lean back, placing my head against his shoulder.

Those few minutes felt like hours. It was me that now was desperate to connect back with Jack. Smelling his smell, shelling my fingers around the curve of his bicep. Loving him. Feeling safe. Holding on to him, knowing that he was everything that Mark wasn't. Wanting to deserve him, appreciate him, and get a handle on what was real. By that time, David was on to his next song, and I hoped so hard that he'd take both Jack and me with him.

seven

The stage lights went down as David finished his last song and exited stage right. Applause ensued and predictably the lights came back on as he reentered to take a final bow. I borrowed David's adulation and felt good. Great, even.

Jack and I made our way out of Radio City and postponed the very popular idea of hailing a cab. We walked and weighed our options. What to do next? We both didn't feel like going home just yet. It was barely eleven and we were spoiled with alternatives. Jack suggested Morgan's. It was nearby and usually filled with friends (his). I was all for it. Ready for whatever the night would bring in a social yet spiteful way. I wanted to continue to be in the company of Jack. Show myself how happy he made me.

We cabbed it after what felt like miles' worth of city blocks. Sharing a cab—the right kind of cab where the driver is coherent, and the car is kept clean—one that is dark but for stagnant city illumination, with the right guy on a rainy night after the right music, is a giant snuggle waiting to happen.

We got comfy and cozy and hugged nice and tight. We were making every light and the slushy sound of rain beneath the tires was perfect.

"Thank you," Jack said. "That was great. Those seats!"

"My pleasure." I smiled. "He's amazing live."

"He really is," Jack said. "Hey . . ." He hesitated. "What happened to you in there? Early on. In the beginning."

"What do you mean?" Looking down and away, I started counting the fringe at the end of my scarf. Pulling it apart. Like splitting the ends of hairs. Carefully. I knew what he meant but hoped that a request for articulation would discourage the conversation.

No dice.

"You got sad. You all but disappeared."

Fourteen. Fifteen. Sixteen.

"Hey," he insisted. "I'm talking to you. What's going on with you?"

"Do you like my scarf?"

Not funny.

"Vivian. C'mon." Frustrated, he shifted himself away from me, encouraging a response.

I dared to meet his eyes. "Nothing is wrong. Nothing was wrong. Honest."

He wasn't buying it.

My insides were fighting to confess, but I never felt confident enough, I guess, to share my experiences with him. From Jack's perspective, I was a completely different woman. Strong, healthy, confident. I was sure he'd never be able to look at me the same way again if he knew about the rest of me. Looking back, I regret that I wasn't honest. I know it would have made things better for us and easier for him.

As (my) luck would have it, the cab pulled over and we were

there before Jack could continue. I put on a very happy face and anxiously awaited every possible distraction.

The bar was full and Jack's mates were crowded in a corner. They were happy to see us. Think *Cheers*.

His friends are good people, as my father would say. A curious mix of under- and overachievers who have only their pasts in common. My big-city reality is quite the contrary—which I dig 'cause that's the interesting part of moving to a new place. I'd left behind all my old associates (except Soph, of course) when I'd come to NYC. I'd started fresh. Now the majority of my friends and our history here feels more like association and circumstance. And no one really has a past unless they elect to tell you so. And that's just the way I like it—meeting people in the "now."

Jack got our drinks and I scoped out Dennis, Matt, Tom, and Lisa. Tom's girlfriend. Finally, a cool wing-woman in the ocean of married couples that was Jack's Sea World. Jack's got five-plus years on me so *Married with Children* ain't just an old show on Fox, ya know?

Lisa was a graduate student. Art History at NYU. She waited tables on the side, which was how she'd met Tom. He and Jack had been dining in her section, and as legend had it, Tom's jaw had nearly dropped when he gazed into the eyes of the girl who was telling them the specials. She was from Maryland. Another "outsider." We got on just fine. She was a vegetarian (her only shortcoming) and always had killer killer jewelry on. Tonight in fact she was wearing these "teardrops," as she called them. Gorg. Three shades of blue. She had beautiful blue eyes and dark brown almost black long hair. Tonight it was up in a knot. Bravo. Very nice.

Tom and Jack grew up side by side all through grade and high school. Literally. Their families lived next door to each other for almost twenty years. He and Andy were Jack's two best friends. Andy was at home tonight. Every few weeks his wife, a nurse, worked the night shift and he minded his three—count 'em, three—kids.

Dennis and Matt excused themselves briskly after spotting two hot blondes, "three o'clock." I complimented Lisa on her earrings; another expert flea market find, she revealed.

"Some people have all the luck," I said and pointed out my naked earlobes.

"They should be ready any day," Jack said.

At their confused looks, I filled in Lisa and Tom:

"The night of my first day at the Web site, Jack took me out for a beautiful dinner . . ."

"Wiseass." Jack laughed. "I picked her up a Big Mac with cheese, chocolate milk shake, and fries . . . her favorite meal."

Table laughs.

"I'm sorry. Where was I . . . before being so rudely inter-rupted." I winked at Jack and continued. "And we're at my place. Dunking fries—in our shakes—a delicacy—I highly recom-mend—kind of like chocolate-covered pretzels but so much better!"

"Noted," Tom said.

"Shhh. Let her finish," Lisa said.

Over the music and the commotion of the setting, I raised my voice earnestly to continue. "And I'm excited and freaked out. Telling Jack all about my day and my coworkers. So happy to be out of my heels and into my sweats."

"I hear that," Lisa said.

"Shhh. Let her finish." Tom cracked himself up with the copy-cat action.

"And Lance Romance here asks me if I want the rest of his fries. The answer he assumes naturally will be a straight-up YES, which it is. Always predictable—when it comes to fast food. But when I reach inside for more, instead of french fries there's this small navy blue velvet box. With salt all over it of course."

"And . . . ," Lisa urged.

"Dum dum du dum . . . ," hummed Tom.

"And," I said over this very awkward moment thanks to Tom, "inside are a pair of diamond studs."

"Uh-uh," Lisa said in a *no-way* tone.

"Uh-huh," I said with a smile.

"I'm surprised it wasn't a ring." Tom raised his beer to Jack. Which he then nearly dropped thanks to Lisa's elbow to his side.

"You're so obnoxious," she said.

"And that's why you love me," he told her. And then they kissed and then Jack and I looked at each other.

"Okay, so Viv—where are they now?" Lisa asked, seeking long-story-short resolution.

"Sorry. We were on holiday, Jamaica, mon, and I put them in the side compartment of my beach bag while I tried my hand at volleyball. When I was through, my first thought was to put my earrings back on and, well, after turning our entire 'campsite' upside down, I had to accept that I'd lost one. I was in a panic, but Jack was so sweet and said it was okay. I had every intention of replacing it even if I had to buy a department store faux pair. But Jack wouldn't hear of it. So, for the last few months I keep hearing how 'the jeweler is working on a replacement pair.' Which is so unnecessary . . . hence the naked lobes."

"Gotcha," said Tom.

"Any day now babe," Jack said.

Lisa and I got up to go to the ladies room. I gave Jack a big smooch before I left. I didn't really care whether he ever replaced the earrings. Just remembering that story was like eating those fries—d-lish!

eight

Another thing I love about Lisa: balls of steel!

With the line for the ladies' room wrapped around the corner, we made a mad dash for the men's room and prayed, well at least I did, that all would be free and clear. (Not a big lover of the random peep show if you know what I mean.)

With no "peeps" in sight, Lisa quickly locks the door behind us and finally lets out the gasp I could just tell she'd been waiting for since Tom's rendition of "The March."

"Admit it," she gushed, "you had to be thinking what I was thinking when you saw that blue box?"

"You're on drugs," I said flatly and got down to business.

Side by side we discussed.

"C'mon, you're kidding me . . . Not even for a moment?"

"I need . . ."

"Here." She passed me some toilet paper. "Now get on with it."

Girls always get down to brass tacks.

"Absolutely not," I said with all honesty. "Not even for a second."

"Really?" She was astounded.

"Really. How's Tom?"

Flush.

"But I would think—" ignoring me.

"Don't," I interrupted.

"Really?"

"Yes. I swear." Knowing full well that she wasn't ready to end the conversation, I did what I could to convince her. "Jack just wouldn't."

"How can you be so sure?" she asked.

" 'Cause I am. Because he knows. We've never even talked about moving in together. And besides, with my job and his freakish schedule . . . we're both good as is."

"Okay. Fine. But let's just say . . . let's just say that it could have been . . . a ring. What then?"

"I can't even imagine. That's it. Really Lisa. It's just so not something he would do. I think you'd get it maybe if you hung around us more. It's just not like that. I mean look, Sophie, you know Sophie, right?"

"Yeah," she said. "The cute little blonde. She works at that magazine, right?"

"Yes. She's my best friend. She heard the very same story and she never asked or even looked twice at me, thinking that it would have been . . . that it could have been—"

Lisa cut me off before I could finish.

"Yeah, but that's because she doesn't hear Jack. She doesn't hear Tom. Talking about you or talking about Jack talking about you."

All this "me" talk was making me very uncomfortable. There wasn't an ounce of me that wanted the details. I realized it and for a moment I felt strange. What girl doesn't enjoy "fishing" from time to time? Was I going out of my mind? Was I in denial? You know what, it was like this: You know when you meet a guy and the first little while is amazing? Over the moon. Tons of phone calls. Great sex. He's lost count of the nights in a row you've spent together and you're simultaneously counting them. Flipping out thinking, *This could be it!!!* He doesn't bring up the guy friends he hasn't seen. You hold hands every chance you get. Does that sound familiar? See, Jack was still that same guy I'd met way back when. Still treated me and treated us like it was the beginning. I never really fretted about an end, 'cause I knew deep down in my heart that if there was to be an end to Jack and me, it would be my doing. And that was why I couldn't bait Lisa for more info.

Jack was the first man, the only man, that I really knew loved me. If I'd let Lisa continue, if I'd gotten the full score from her, I might have had to tell her, too. I might've had to tell her what I was scared of when all was said and done. What I didn't think I could admit. Honestly, I felt as though I wasn't good enough for him. I couldn't love him the way he loved me and I wondered when he was going to figure that out.

Rifling through her makeup bag, Lisa paused. "He loves you, Vivian. (pause) He loves you."

Uch.

"So be ready for it, girl, because it's coming."

"You're out of your mind," I said and wished the dryer would hurry the hell up!

"No babe. You are."

Nine

It was decided early on (year one of the Web site) that the corporate execs and corporate planners would "just let me be me" and they wouldn't try to "program" my life for the site. But slowly it surfaced (year two of the Web site) that there were two minds and two minds only that shared the same point of view when it came to the positioning and promotion of the Web site. But the millions of minions in the middle felt as though I should grow to become "somebody." The "everywoman," aka me, would start out average and evolve into someone extraordinary as millions watched adoringly on-line. *Extraordinary*, in their book, was defined as a "pop-culture phenomenon." Bubble gum of the millennium that would lose its flavor after everyone got mad rich. Bubble gum that would be spit out once it lost its flavor. And how were they aiming to do that? Well, it beat the hell out of me. Perhaps they dreamed of phat endorsement deals, cameos here and there, a high-profile man of the moment . . . we all know how it goes.

I wasn't really defiant, because who of us would not, even

for a moment, enjoy the high price of fame if we could pick it up for a Costco-like price? (Chew on that.) I was just always pretty sure I wouldn't measure up. I mean seriously, what entity is based on ordinary and familiar, really, anyway? And that's truly how I saw myself. I was, and am, ordinary. Look, I've never been one to sell myself short, but if they were looking for a viva-glam diamond in the rough, I was certainly going to be their "forgazi." Sure, Kelly Clarkson is as American Pie as they come, but here's the catch: The girl can SING! You dig?

I could feel that pressure for a while. Coworkers not really getting that it was okay that their meal ticket was donning last season's shoes, or was dating a part-time civil servant, or was still more comfortable seated in a movie theater on a fabulous Thursday night than she was at that reservationless hot spot.

It was the vision of the Web site's founder that I be just as I am. Me (or whoever it was who got the gig when it all came down to it). And I think everyone else signed on assuming that the rest would just come naturally. It was, if you think about it, a pretty radical concept. The cybercelebrity who didn't take her clothes off, didn't bear a famous last name, never won a gold medal or statuette, and had not an ounce of notoriety beforehand. So I get what all the confusion was about, looking back at least.

It was one argument too many, late on a Friday, when I realized that things were about to get interesting. Interesting because I was about to shed my insecure coat and try on something a little more empowering.

We were in a staff meeting, developing a concept for a (hopefully) upcoming eight-page layout in a national magazine. A concept that would spawn perks for our users and a presence that would eventually transcend print and end up online and at retail. The thing was, we were very close to signing a very big advertiser. A kick-ass concept for an ad with potential would do the trick, we hoped. And if landed, the pressure would be taken off sales, which would then alleviate the pressure from every other department. A deal that if done and done right, would make the rest of the calendar year a breeze and likewise assure that our Web site would not be featured on the always updated "dot bomb" list.

I had a great idea for a "road trip" theme. But others had their own takes and weren't so excited about mine. They barely listened to my proposal before moving on to others and forgetting mine ever existed. I would have just chalked it up to misdirection on my part—after all, what the heck did I know about it? But their ideas felt forced and phony to me. And because I knew I'd have to participate, given my role, I wanted to make sure that it all felt right. That it felt like me. There was bitterness, lots of it, when I voiced my concern that their ideas weren't "me." Like most of corporate America, people at FAI can be freakish and competitive and are always trying to cut to the head of the line. So there were accusations a-flying and rumors a-milling that I was saying no basically because the idea wasn't mine. And another thing about corporate America: In die-hard situations people feel the need to articulate publicly for the sake of being heard and going on record. (At least when we were all in junior high school, we were talking behind other people's backs, wary of the repercussions. Not so in the real world.) So it was acceptable in staff meetings to cut me up, so long as "no offense Vivian" began or ended every insult.

Drew pulled me over after an exceptionally bitter display. "Vivian. Let's figure this out tonight. I hear what you're saying but I feel like unless we demonstrate your idea and make it a physical thing, you're toast."

"Okay," I said warily. One, because "support" such as this

was still a rare thing at the time. And two, well, because the idea of a Friday night with Drew sounded interesting. It didn't feel like work. I mean, if nothing else perhaps we'd forge a friendship. I was interested in this guy. It wasn't like I had developed this huge mad crush, I mean we both had significant others and as I think I've said before, I found him to be a bit girly. But underneath all of our sparring over the past weeks, Drew intrigued me—and, well, intrigue can be a hot thing.

"This way we can present it fresh Monday morning," he said.

"Yeah," I said, still a bit taken aback. "Cool."

"All right. So meet me in my office at six." His friendliness felt odd for him, I think, too.

"You got it."

He started to walk past me but turned back and asked, "Can I get you anything? What do you eat?"

Sheryl passed us, easily over that monster of a meeting and very ready to get her weekend started. "Good night," she said to us both with an elevated voice—almost presenting it as a question.

" 'Night," I said.

Sheryl winked my way and, I must say, it felt very peculiar. Office antics other than those with Gabe and Carolyn when I was back at VH1 were few and far between here at the Web site. I turned to answer Drew:

"Oh. Whatever is fine."

No. No. No! That wasn't just me with that answer—was it? Hang on. Still, there was no way that he'd read into it that I'm a "whatever" kinda girl, right? For me, the gal with an infamous appetite, if my memory serves me correctly, there's never been an occasion when I've been agreeable and low-maintenance in the food department . . . this, my immediate and surprisingly instinctual remark, was HUGE. And geez, then what did that all mean? With an hour to kill, this quandary would serve as just the right amount of self-analysis to pass the time away.

Hmmmmmm.

In the end I chalked my unnatural food response up to politeness. Drew was being cool. He was setting himself up to be my confidant and partner in crime and he was going out of his way. Why make him jump through hoops to meet my fast-food whims? My response was one of consideration. Yup, total consideration. The fact that Mickey D's was downstairs and around the corner was irrelevant.

Moving on . . .

ten

Back in the confines of my office, I first called Sophie. We had planned to meet for happy hour, and in light of recent events it wasn't gonna happen. She was disappointed upon hearing the news. No worries, she wasn't down on me, but she was now in desperate need of a replacement wing-woman as there was a certain someone she was planning to run into. You know, in one of those brilliantly planned coincidences we girls like to pull. She asked to be forwarded to May and I happily obliged. (I loved that she had adopted May into our circle of friends. It's fun when "the mutuals" get along.)

I next rang Jack and left a message on his machine.

"Hi Jack. Just wanted to say hi. I'm working late tonight. I'll call you later. 'Bye."

Why? I have no idea actually. It's not like we were meant to be seeing each other this evening. But much like my "whatever" dinner comment, I was all off guard and making something out of nothing. Covering my tracks as though I were hiding something shameful. Quite the contrary but something told me to do so. Weird.

I popped by the ladies' room on my way to Drew's office. Brushed my teeth, put the now haglike hair in a pony, and schmeared a bit of gloss on my pasty, overworked, underlubed lips.

I entered and sat on the very modern minimalist black leather sofa that he had positioned just opposite his desk. His office felt more like a bachelor pad. (I wouldn't be surprised if the whole space had been feng-shui'd. It had that kind of vibe.) A curious orchid sat atop the windowsill behind me, casually leaning over my shoulder as though it were eavesdropping. A straight guy with an orchid? Hmmm. Drew was on speakerphone. Sounded like he was shooting the shit with another one of his supercool friends. All chuckles and agreements as though their whole lives were private jokes. Spare me. In an instant I got up, did the *one-minute* finger thing, and traipsed back to my office. Having a conversation with myself all the while. It consisted mostly of, *Get a grip, Vivian. This is too-cool-for-school Drew. What the devil could you have been thinking? You don't like him. Get real. Get real.*

I had a trusty drawer in my file cabinet reserved for "personals":

1. A now-too-tight bra that I forgot doesn't belong in the dryer
2. A pair of heels that looked hot in theory but were devil incarnate on the feet
3. A bottle of wine sent as a congratulatory gift from a client
4. A smelly white tank top that I realized a few hours too late was smelly

5. An ugly logo'd cheap freebie messenger bag from an after-work event
6. A novel I bought at Barnes & Noble 'cause it was absurdly thick and had a cool cover that I thought would be impressive if I managed to ever finish it
7. An old pair of velourish navy Juicy sweatpants
8. A pair of whitish gray-cobalt blue cheap-o rubber thongs for pedicures

BINGO!

Off with the tired tight trousers!

Fitted by now wrinkled broadcloth blouse be gone!

Adios boo-tays!

I returned several minutes later in a black shrunken cotton cardigan that I'd been in the habit of hanging over my chair. A day-old white tank (it's all good, not the smelly one), my cozy Juicy sweats, and my cheapy flip-flops. Ahhhhhhhhhhh. Rejuvenated and ready to work and above all else—realistic.

Now, where were we?

Upon my reentering, Drew didn't comment on the new attire and instead got right down to business.

"The thing is, Vivian, you've got to keep in mind that when you present an idea, one that applies to you directly, it comes off in a different way than if it were someone else talking about the very same thing."

I didn't get what he meant and it must've been apparent by the serious *huh* expression embedded in the wrinkles of my scrunched forehead.

"You're too laid back for these people. It's not that you're not professional, because you are, don't get me wrong, but I think everyone is so used to a more businesslike approach." Drew made his points rather effortlessly. It was nice. It would've been pretty easy for him to come off condescending if his tone had been slightly different. The more he talked, the more obvious it was that he was right, and I found his advice to be invaluable. Enter meticulous mental notes.

He continued, "I would love to see you keep your warmth, that charm, but come better equipped. Do you know what I mean?"

"Yeah. I do actually."

"And that's where I come in."

I had never listened so intently in all my life. I honed in on his every movement and hung on his every word. It was as if I were squinting to make something out in the distance.

"Are you okay?" he asked.

"Fine. Why?" Still squinting.

He laughed. "You just look like you're in pain. Do you wear contacts?"

Embarrassed yet headstrong, "Quit it!" I urged. "I'm listening. Go on."

"From now on, I think you and I and maybe Sheryl should schedule premeets before the larger staff meetings. Maybe two days prior? Review the agendas. Get your feedback. This way, we can fine-tune your ideas, provide visual aids, stats, and get everyone's attention."

"I would love that."

"It's obvious you know what you're talking about. I mean, you, more than anyone else around here, understands our audience. She's you. You know how you want to be marketed to. Between you and me, how can Stan really relate to our target market? Watching *Sex and the City* doesn't exactly make you an expert on women?"

"Thanks," I agreed, "and well, I'm sure you know how I feel about Stan."

He gave me a conciliatory smile and continued. "I think that 'road trip' idea you had today was phenomenal. But it needs to be spelled out. I think you need to present the overall concept going forward and then both myself and Sheryl need to back it up."

"Got it," I said. Inside I was beaming. His thumbs-up gave me an unexpected rush.

Drew had ordered Chinese and it came some twenty minutes later. Wonton soup, pork fried rice, and General Tso's chicken (who is General Tso by the way?)—nicely done. We talked through the "road trip" concept until it was bone dry. Together we canvassed the 'Net for images we could grab that would help with the presentation. We came up with taglines and contests, places on the Web site where promotional elements could be tied in. It was fun actually.

His girlfriend called at about ten P.M. and until she noted it, we hadn't even realized how late it actually was. She promptly asked to be taken off speaker and I leafed through a sharp photography book that was placed neatly alongside that nosy flower as if to make it look like I wasn't listening. 'Cause I fully fully was.

That's an odd concept, come to think of it. "Make it look like you're not listening." What could you possibly do to casually appear as though you weren't hearing something? How does reading a book turn your hearing off? I know. This is really neither here nor there so I'll stop pondering the useless and continue. My bad.

Their conversation was terse. So much so that it was basically a buzz kill. I think he was a bit embarrassed, actually, as his tone with her so contrasted to the tone of our evening. I mean meeting, sorry. They hung up after a few minutes and he apologized for the distraction.

"Please," I urged. "It's fine."

"She's great BUT she's a bit of a control freak," he confessed.

"It's okay, Drew. You don't need to explain." Even though I was so hoping he would!

"It's fine if she's on a shoot and can't get away. But if I work late on a night that she's not . . ." I was floored that he was getting so personal. Usually mature guys whom I don't know very well aren't this open. And it was odd because his tone was very matter-of-fact. It wasn't registering like a complaint. Nor was his remark conveyed in a dramatic or sarcastic tone. It was as if I had asked him what the weather was like outside and he'd said, *Partly cloudy with a chance of rain.* Regardless, he was divulging and I loved it. Nobody's perfect and it was a breath of fresh air to see this side of Drew.

"She got me that orchid," he said with a grin. "Insisted it live in here."

"Uh-huh," I said and grinned back. I'm sure my raised eyebrow gave away my initial thoughts.

"I knew it! It's gay, right? What straight guy has an orchid in his office? I'm thirty-four and single. I have a rottweiler and a Harley-Davidson, for Christ's sake."

We both started cracking up. Finally Drew was being real! It was a *huge* breath of fresh air.

"You take it," he said.

"What, the orchid?"

"Yes."

"I couldn't." (Yes, I so could!)

"Just take it. I feel like an idiot every time someone walks in here."

"Yeah, we all call you 'orchid boy' behind your back."

"Really?" he said. Astonished, offended, and amused all at once.

"No."

eleven

Yeah, so like I said: That evening, sorry, meeting (what is wrong with me tonight), was a turning point of sorts. I realized that there was a softer side to even the coldest of cats and, simultaneously, I learned to embrace the inner and awkward puppy dog in me. Granted, my stint at VH1 was a definite notch in my belt, but the pressures of being the featured performer at a Web site that bore my name, well, that was a whole other animal. And although I had a sneaking suspicion that I knew what I was talking about, that Friday night was like an assisted revelation. I realized that I might very well know what I was saying—but how I said it was very very key.

The Monday following, Drew and I rocked the house. The Sunday night before, my nervous energy had gone awry, and Jack had borne the brunt of it, the poor thing, assuring me that it would "all be fine."

His quick confidence in my abilities felt unfounded. I mean, how did he know—really? And his "I just do" reply made me crazy. Not in a boiling-bunnies kinda way. More like resentment in the form of a mumble that he forced me to annunciate:

"How—would—you—know?" I repeated for the sake of clarity.

In my mind I was referring to the fact that he had no experience in the world that I worked in. He knew nothing of Bekka, Brooke, and Jenni, the three "witches of work-wick" as I so affectionately called them. Who greeted me with forced smiles upon every sighting and canvassed me head to toe whenever they thought I wasn't looking. Three women whom I had to force myself not to ask if they ever got laid, who were wound so tight and just so stuck up that they found it arduous to answer my (seldom asked) questions audibly and instead formed a habit of sour-facial-remark responses that I had no choice but to learn to translate and actually react to. And how about the spectacles that were my weekly staff meetings; standing room only more often than not, where my life was critiqued and my responses criticized? I mean, even as things got easier they were still hard, you know? So really, how could Jack be so sure???

Much like a complicated recipe, it wasn't long before Jack learned to let me marinate when the going got tough rather than fault me for my ugly nervous-energy/self-doubting addiction. 'Cause as much as I hated it—all the pressure—it somehow fueled me. Honestly, had I had an easy breezy weekend, that weekend, consciously agreeing with Jack all along, well then I would have had nothing to "fight" or "spin" into something positive—i.e., a kick-ass pitch that would floor my colleagues. You know, I guess different things work for different people. I just happen to be one of the weird ones who thrives under the pressure that I so think I hate.

Anyway, all that aside, that was another reason why we love Jack. 'Cause he got that part of me and just let me be. Rarely taking personal offense at my distraction once I was on his clock (but I'd get better, before I got worse).

Back to my story: Scores of people congratulated me after that Monday-morning meeting. Personally and through e-mails. It was genius. And after we made it official, and actually got the "road trip" deal some few weeks later, I received a phone call from the founder of the site. It was with quiet confidence that she said she was "proud of me"; a quick conversation that practically validated all the time, effort, and energy that was "the process."

Very cool.

Drew was biking through Baja with his babe when it all became official. I was bummed that he wasn't around to celebrate what he was practically responsible for. (Or could I have been peeved that it wasn't my big bum on the back of his bike?) Either way, May, Sophie, and I treated ourselves to a corporate-sponsored dinner at Next Door Nobu. Fabulous!

May was over everything:

> Over-joyed that our company had landed such a big
>   account.
> Over-the-moon that it was the "road trip" idea that had
>   tipped the scale.
> Over-Stan, seriously, for being such an "affected
>   asshole"—her words, not mine.

"You would think he'd 'get it,' you know?" she quipped, racing through her sake. "He's got such a big job there and I feel like he lives on a totally different planet!"

"Easy girl . . ." I cautioned. Her adrenaline could be scary at times.

"You know exactly what I mean, Vivian. And honestly, you

guys, if he sends me on one more errand to Prada Sport, I think I'm going to hand him my resignation along with his receipts!"

"He does NOT make you do that?" Sophie said, shocked.

"Please, half my week is spent in Soho." Another shot of sake gone.

Sophie looked my way and because I'd been friends with this girl since grade school it was pretty easy to get where her mind was going: Shopping, if even for another, wasn't exactly the worst thing in the world.

So I tried to rephrase in Sophie-terms: "May was not hired to be Stan's errand girl. She's brilliant and has the most amazing ideas, but she's too busy baby-sitting to actually execute any of them, ever. And when she politely calls him on it, he apologizes and basically picks up where he's left off, what, May, like some two days later?"

"Yup," she said, defeated. "And the thing is, I don't want to quit. I love it. The site. Vivian. I totally believe in it. But I mean, what am I really learning? What am I really doing?"

She was so right and it sucked.

"I'm sorry V," she said. "This is such a big night for you. I hate to be a buzz kill . . ."

"Don't be ridiculous," I insisted. "We're your friends. What good are we if you can't talk to us?"

"Well, there's always the free dinners," she joked. But it wasn't really that funny. Every ounce of me wanted to help May. "Tattletale," if you will, and help her get repositioned, working alongside someone who would value her and teach her. But I knew that would only backfire on the two of us. If she was going to get anywhere with Stan, she was going to have to do it on her own.

Sophie offered her insight. "When I first started at the magazine, the first year, I was EVERYONE'S assistant. And if on the off chance someone was not all that comfortable taking advantage of the situation, they still never went out of their way to be nice, include me, nothing."

May looked my way for validation. "It's true, May," I said.

"So finally, when I was at my bottom, fully thinking that I'd never progress and never get out from under the minutiae of my job, I kinda flew off the handle and just said no. Or maybe I said, 'Yes, I do mind actually.' It was something like that. When I didn't care anymore and had not a single expectation, *then* I stuck up for myself and drew a line." (I was so proud of Sophie—it was like she was my daughter and she'd ridden her two-wheeler for the very first time. *Well said, Sophie,* I thought to myself. *Bravo.*)

"And they didn't fire you, I take it," May asked with a hint of optimism.

"Nope. They promoted me some three months later and in the interim, left me the hell alone."

"Nice," I added.

"Well they did!" Sophie insisted.

"I know Soph! I just love that story."

"It's true. And it's weird," she continued. "I almost feel like I made it worse on someone else, you know? For passing the *shit-on-me* torch. Because people like that have to have someone else to put down. It's too bad really, but that's just the way it is."

"So do you think I should stand up to Stan?" May asked.

"Definitely," Sophie said.

"Vivian? You think so, too?"

"Yeah May, I do. You need to set boundaries. Serious boundaries. There's no way he's going to let you go. No way. I mean really, what would he say? *She got sick of shopping for me?* He would never. It's just that this time you need to bluff, explaining very matter-of-factly that you'll walk."

"High stakes," Sophie warned.

"But so worth it," I said.

There was a quick silence. May was cataloging our strong words of advice. We were like some coltish *go-for-it* tag team. Weathered rookies.

"It's all one big game, isn't it?" she surmised.

"Yup," we said.

Then we each said, "Jinx."

And again, "Jinx."

And again, "Jinx!"

Laughing like two huge dorks but not caring. It wasn't until May raised her small sake shot glass—to which we did the same—that we got ahold of ourselves.

"To me!" May proclaimed.

"To justice!" Sophie said.

"To tomorrow," I noted.

"To tomorrow," May repeated and gave us both a shared *oh-my-God* expression.

"To tomorrow," we all said.

They each sucked down their sake. I would have, too, but I spilled mine all over my wrist.

twelve

May lost her momentum: Stan came down with a case of the flu—a pretty nasty one at that—and was out sick the rest of that week. But I for one wasn't worried. I knew she'd follow through when the right moment revealed itself. And knowing Stan, that moment would come sooner rather than later.

The office took on a very "ding-dong the witch is dead" Dorothy-esque quality in Stan's absence. After being sick, he had business on the West Coast and took the "witches of work-wick" with him. So without a substitute teacher in sight, there was a new levity at the office that encouraged both productivity and this strange, college-mixer-type mischievousness.

Antics and rituals started taking over. From pizza parties in the boardrooms to "artwork" in the bathrooms. Noteworthy gossip pages were tacked to the walls of the copy areas; people began hanging out and working after normal business hours 'cause it was actually becoming fun. My company was developing a personality and that suited me just fine.

I started kicking back in Sheryl's office with Marni and May. We'd turn on the cheesiest light FM radio station and 'fess up to truths that surfaced upon every sappy eighties love song. We even got May to admit that she'd hooked up with Sean, this hot guy in our systems department. Boy, did he fix hers! (Seriously, don't tell her I told you—she'd kill me!) Together we all opened up, confessed, and collaborated: dysfunctional families, nightmare bosses, phony friends and New Year's resolutions that had already gone awry. It was obvious to me that although we were all so different, as workingwomen we all just wanted the same simple things. Achievements, acknowledgments, independence and yes, of course, great love.

The thing is, in the months and years that I would get to know my friends at the office, I would also get to know thousands of women online, too. As the "connector" I could see everything so clearly. The office was short-staffed and stretched thin, so I was always doing something: answering e-mails, reading bulletin board posts, traveling to city after city, meeting fans of the site. So, constantly pressed for time, I had no choice but to dismiss the bullshit and focus on the meaning of each interaction. It was the only way to handle it all. And because the World Wide Web is all about quick forms of expression and because my time meeting new people was always clocked, women would just get right down to it . . . and so would I. The honesty of it all fully rocked my world. And in time, my clarity was nearly palpable.

I came to carry around this awareness of camaraderie, and it enhanced my life in ways I can't even describe. I could see it. I could hold it. And soon I became a full-fledged girl's girl. I would have never imagined that I'd have schools of girlfriends. Truth be told I'd never even wanted them. I was never open to it before. We give ourselves such a bad rap!

I was the girl with all the guy friends. It was easier I thought. But that's not the case if you're open to it. It's so not the case.

Backdrops—age, race, religion—are just here to fuck with us. Every woman can get the other. It's that simple.

But governing my revelation was a whole other thing. I was this close to becoming a mushy feministlike Hare Krishna . . .

Women everywhere, stop what you're doing, turn to the girl next to you, and get to know her. Ask her how she's doing. Ask her if she's happy. Disclose your fears!!!

Oh please! I came to the conclusion that my vantage point was a privilege unique to me. We all know now that we can't change our men. So how the hell was I going to change my women? Instead I hoped to be able to filter my feelings through different media and, if nothing else, be able to reap the rewards in my own life. Bottom line, if you had told me five years ago that I would feel this connected to the world in which I lived I would have thought you a Froot Loop and had you for breakfast. I mean, really.

I want so bad to be specific right now but I know it will come across in a weird way. So trust me on this: We're all lost and lonely in certain ways. We are never as we appear; a subtle gesture that comes out of compassion, interest, and humility can be a breath of fresh air.

There. I've said my piece. File it somewhere.

thirteen

A lounge-y lounge called Luvas opened right around the corner from my office and soon became my own personal haunt. It was decadently dark—illuminated only by lit cigarettes and a single but enormous crystal chandelier in the ceiling's center. It was a long and mysterious rectangle of a room. In its middle was the bar. Another rectangle. Retro in feel and luxurious, it was solid mahogany. Rich and romantic. Sleek and glazed to perfection. I wouldn't have been surprised to find a Ralph Lauren label nailed to it somewhere inside. The plush velvet stools that surrounded it were a happy dark blue color. They were more like chairs designed for basketball players. (I have this thing about bar stools . . . I get pissy when they don't have backs. Go figure.) Placed all about the bar were sordid short-stemmed roses in pear-shaped mini modern silver vases, tarnished, as you would expect, just right.

Along Luvas's perimeter were berry-colored seats and sofas. Nostalgic and exaggerated. Too big for their own britches. In fabrics that felt like fall. This was cool: The walls, exposed brick, were covered with black-and-white photos of couples, families, and friends through the ages. Everyone looked different but everyone looked pleased. Housed in new and old frames, tarnished, too, in golds and silvers. Crisp blacks. Modern and vintage. The crowded montage felt more like wallpaper and gave the place a vibe like no other. They were everywhere and, rather than in the air, love was on the walls. Give me a second and I'll explain.

As you'd walk to the back of the lounge, your eye would come across two pool tables, side by side like fingers. Onlookers were provided for with pairs of leather club chairs. Free to speculate on who would beat whom, who was with whom, who was doing whom, etc. If you looked up, you'd see the DJ spinning from a makeshift balcony covered in vines. If Romeo and Juliet had had a skybox it probably would have looked like that.

I loved Luvas 'cause I always felt that it "got" me. If I went in there all happy, it felt happy. If I walked in angry, it was on my side. It was romantic when I was romantic and sad when I was sad. Mysterious, thought-provoking, yet painfully optimistic in a very wise sort of way.

If you haven't caught on by now, I'm big on environments.

With my waitressing days behind me—thank God, an utterly thankless profession—I was curious about the stories that cloaked this staff. What was their deal? Why were they there? Where were they going? There were, of course, the token pretty boys and girls who manned the bar and toyed with the patrons. The angry cocktail waitresses with tired eyes and pale skin who looked like they'd been on a bender. The gangly busboys who spent their tiny paychecks updating their instruments rather than on a bag of much-needed groceries. Quiet and shy, they kept to themselves in worn-out saggy pants that used to fit them. And then there was the mysterious manager, who pretty much kept to himself, too. I always wanted to tell him how much I dug the place but his whole demeanor screamed, *Why bother?*

Like I said, I was becoming a permanent fixture. Especially after they implemented their menu. Luvas was also a five-star finger-food establishment. Perrrrrrrfect. And I never got bored there, 'cause there was always eye candy, great music, and that vibe. While pretending to be interested in conversations, I could always count on a new photo I hadn't seen yet that warranted analysis to the right, to the left, or just above the person I was talking with. What, like you don't know what I mean? C'mon now.

And those photos . . . man, they totally threw me for a loop. Usually old photos of people I've never known kind of freak me out. They get me all sad. (Especially when they're for sale at flea markets and such. What's that about anyway? Can you imagine your treasured family album one day lying, stuffed like a sardine, in a one-dollar BUY ME trunk? Yuck.) But it was so not the case in this current setting. Interesting, I never paid too much attention to the men in the pictures. Maybe 'cause I couldn't relate. I'll never pretend to know what a guy is thinking. But the women—well, that was another story entirely. Their expressions were all so familiar, almost daunting at times. Forever peaceful. Forever happy. It was like a giant freeze-frame where their futures didn't matter. They forever lived in the present. Ignorance is bliss maybe? The photos oozed with optimism. Maybe that's why I liked them so much.

I remember as a kid, I'd made my mom decorate my room with everything Snow White. I had Snow White sheets and blankets. Snow White storybooks and stickers. Two night-lights even! And I loved my cheery seven dwarfs, tiny miniatures that I lined up, in the proper order I'll have you know, on a shelf above my dresser. On my nightstand I had this plastic slash ceramic statuette slash lamp. All Snow White. One year my mom got creative and framed Snow White illustrations on my wall within thin, pretty yellow borders. Oh, hang on; I mustn't forget my Snow White sleeping bag!

Sure, I grew out of Snow White eventually, but at the time my room became one giant fairy tale. 'Cause I always knew that after all the bullshit and the whole poison incident, Snow White lived happily ever after and had tons of guy friends, too! I never did hear of Snow White having any domestic disputes, her man leaving her for Betty Boop or anything like that. She never hit the bottle or had an ungrateful kid write some scathing unauthorized autobiography. She had the consummate happy ending, despite a rocky start. The perfect room. There was nothing to fear.

Luvas, for the moment, kept me in the present, and the photos helped me live in the now. Living in the now allows you to forget about the past and not worry about the future. Much like my girl Snow, I guess.

That's a funny name, *Snow White*, of course.

So I was big on the place. Very big. And it was cool 'cause no one really ever caught on to how much time I really spent there. Not to worry, I wasn't some sad wino who shut the place down every night. What I mean is, it became a great spot to go with my work friends. It was chic enough that Sophie really dug it. And Jack liked it there, too. I mean really, how seldom does that happen?

Jack actually REALLY dug the place. Which came as quite a shock. "The bigger the shithole the better the bar!"—that was Jack's motto. Whatever. (But between you and me, I had a sneaking suspicion that he might. Like it, that is. 'Cause it had a very guy feel to it.) Anyway, he started hanging out there, too. Sometimes, when I'd call him from my parents' place or if I was out to dinner with girls, he'd tell me that he'd gone there with some friends. To play pool and stuff. I thought that was cute.

A whole mess of us from the office went there one night. It was Marni's birthday. (Her fiancé surprised her and showed up—so sweet; they had gotten engaged a few weeks prior.) We did the cake thing and the collective-office-present thing and, one by one, people said their good-byes and went home or whatever. May, Drew, and I were the last ones there. We talked shop, disputed conflicting opinions about movie X, album Y, and restaurant Z. Drew excused himself to make a phone call outside, and May and I agreed that he was so definitely calling "But." May then, rather matter-of-factly, asked me if I wanted to be alone with Drew, which was a very strange question and totally caught me off guard. It made me feel like I was about to cheat, that I was already cheating, on my boyfriend, as crazy as that may sound.

"What kind of question is that?" I said defensively.

"What?" she, too, said defensively.

"Why would I want to be alone with Drew? Are you kidding me?"

"I don't know," she said. "Kinda feels like three's a crowd," she murmured.

"So then let's ask him to leave!" I laughed.

And she laughed. And then she asked me to "forget I even mentioned it."

"Forgotten," I said.

Drew came back to the bar.

"So what are you guys drinking?" he asked. Lifting his little behind from his chair to grab his wallet.

"You know . . ." May said. "I'm gonna get going. I've got a lot of shopping to do tomorrow."

☺

I was shocked. I wanted to laugh and I was a wee bit peeved, too, but before I could think of what to say to May, if anything, Drew chimed in.

"Still?" he asked. Implying that Stan was still abusing the privilege of having a personal assistant.

"Don't even get me started," she urged.

With that, May bounced from her chair, threw her coat on, asked how much she owed for her drinks. To which Drew gave her a *please, don't even try to pay for your own drinks* face so she put her bag over her shoulder and told us she'd see us tomorrow.

"Yup, see you tomorrow." I said and in such a way that May would pick up on the fact that she was toast (yet still nonchalantly enough that Drew would never in his right mind think that she or I or we had planned her quick exit).

There was an awkward silence at first. A fun awkward silence.

"How's But?" I asked.

"Who?" he said.

"But."

"Who's But?" He was confused.

"She's great But . . . things are good But . . . we have a lot of fun But . . ."

"I get it. Very funny." Yeah, he caught on rather quickly and, I could tell, he found my remarks to be somewhat amusing.

"What are you trying to say, Vivian?" He smiled.

"Nothing," I teased.

"No, it's cool. I get it. I get it." Pause . . . "So tell me then, how's Jake?"

"Jack."

"Right, right. Jack. How's he doin'?"

"Fine. What's your point?" I don't much like when situations get reversed.

"I don't really have a point." Smug, he sipped his beer. "Do you mind if I smoke?" he asked but only for the sake of being po-lite. You could tell that he was going to light up regardless of my answer. And if you don't mind me saying so, he looked as if he needed one.

"Light up . . . if you must."

Interestingly enough, he didn't have any of his own. He bummed off the bartender.

By now it was obvious to both of us that our respective rela-tionships each had its own unique set of issues, so we got past the *who's-in-a-more-screwed-up-relationship* showdown and slowly opened up.

We both had dogs whom we fully loved in a very "crazy dog owner" kind of way. Much like if we had kids we shared bragging rights and swapped "awwwwwwwww-ish" stories. He also talked a lot about his older sister who, with two young children, had just left her husband. He'd been messing around with another woman. The entire family, evidently, was very broken up about it. She was living with their parents now and unsure of what she'd do next. There was the custody issue and something about Drew's dad. How he'd fronted money for his brother-in-law to start his business. It sounded like a real mess.

Not wanting to leave him out in the cold and not because I was vying for who had a more screwed-up family, but because I just felt like it, I told Drew about my oldest brother, Simon, whom my family doesn't even communicate with anymore. (Long story—buy book one or just take my word for it. Let's just say they didn't "approve" of his bride and leave it at that.) And now Simon has a kid, whom my folks have never even met. Nightmare.

I think that my first "truth" was a little more fucked up than Drew could handle actually. He didn't even know how to respond. Divorce was one thing. Excommunication was another, I gathered. I was also getting the feeling that Drew was the kind of guy who never really had personal drama in his life. Lucky. He seemed like one of those rare suburban kids—like the one whose house you liked to have sleep-overs at and not because the parents were away for the weekend or because their pantry had a Willy Wonka thing going on. But because the family was close and unassuming. Beaver-Cleaverish. Who knows.

Strangely enough, I didn't have a problem getting real with Drew. And I don't really know why 'cause if I told you that there was a part of him that I didn't still find intimidating, I'd be lying. I hadn't even told May about Simon and Jack always knew better than to bring it up. Odd, right?

A guy and a girl got up from a sofa set near the bar, leaving prime real estate up for grabs. I pointed them out to Drew and suggested we move. I sprawled out on the small burgundy love seat. Drew took the lonely red chair.

He started talking about a bachelor party in Vegas he'd be going to in the coming weeks for a fraternity brother blah blah blah. I could so see Drew as a frat boy! And I told him so and he got offended—momentarily.

"Well, I so see you in college, Vivian. Purposefully not pledging a sorority just because." I felt like he was mimicking me a little.

"Because why?" I was curious. He was right. I never had.

"Because you thought you knew what it was all about. Thought you were too cool for that."

"Thought?"

"Yes. And I bet you would have liked it, too."

"And why is that?" He was so sure he had me pegged.

"It's obvious, Vivian."

"To you maybe." I was getting antsy and aggravated.

"The Web site . . . your Web site."

I interrupted, "Our Web site."

"You're right. Our Web site. Excuse me. It's the ultimate soror-ity. Do you not see that?"

I thought it over while he finished his point. All of which I pretty much tuned out, but in the silence of my own mind, I ac-tually agreed with him on some level. Yes, the Web site did share a lot of the same elements if it were to be compared to the best example of what a sorority had to offer. Only because I'm sure I'm not the only one who's heard some of the lesser-than-lovely stories about them, ya know.

But on another level, me not pledging or whatever had less to do with interest and preconceived notions than it did, I'm em-barrassed to say, with what options existed for me at the time.

Mark . . . he would have had none of it.

Reflecting on my college years and what I did and did not do during them was not a head I wanted to be in. Quickly I found a fetching photo to the right of Drew's elbow to stare through. It had an *I Love Lucy* fifties quality to it. Guy and girl pausing during what looked like a cheeky checkerboard picnic. Facing the camera and seated on the floor, guy had arm around girl. Guy was in profile, his hair slicked back sorta greased-lightning-ish, and he was whispering something to girl. Girl was giggling, her smile wide and bright. She had on very dark lipstick for a fun Saturday afternoon in the park but that was her prerogative. She was wearing a dress, but it looked more like a short-sleeved fitted blouse and a skirt. She was barefoot; her pointy black flats were in the foreground. She looked younger than him.

Drew was still recollecting frat life.

The guy seemed relaxed and the girl, giddy. What was that

all about really? I wondered if she'd trashed the picture some months later and oddly, decades down the road, it'd ended up here.

Enough.

"I'm gonna go," I told him.

Interrupted, Drew looked at his watch and then at me. "Okay. Wow. It's almost midnight."

"Yeah, it's getting late." I gathered my things and got up. Drew was still seated. And a cocktail waitress set down another cold beer. Before he could say anything I leaned down and gave him a kiss on his cheek.

"I'll see you tomorrow," I said and left.

Normally I would have been concerned with my coltish exit. But that night it was the last thing on my mind.

fourteen

The next morning, back at the ranch, the one where I work, my first order of business was to make sure to see my former friend May. Coffee and newspaper in hand, I marched right over to her desk.

"What was that all about?" I said to match her welcoming oops look. "Seriously, that was really unnecessary. Why did you bolt last night?"

"To be honest, I was tired. I wasn't even gonna go but it was Marni's birthday and then there were the chocolate cupcakes, so . . . But after a while I'd had enough. Drew and I aren't friends, you two are, and I was all about getting home and channel-surfing. Really, Vivian, I was just teasing. I would have skipped out even if there were a dozen of us left. I was only playing with you."

"Fine. But you freaked me out," I said. "I got all self-conscious. The last thing I would want is for Drew or for anyone else to think I was into him."

"I'm soorrrrrrry. Okay?"

"Okay." *No harm done*, I thought to myself. *Why make a mountain—*

"But . . ." May interrupted my thoughts.

"But what?"

"But, I'd be remiss if I didn't say this: I think you need to think about why my harmless little joke got you so bent out of shape. If it were that unrealistic, the whole idea of you guys having some one-on-one time, you would have just let it roll off your back . . ."

"He's got a girlfriend, I've got Jack . . ."

May's desk was just outside Stan's office. He walked past us and gave May an *I need you*—now look, which was my cue to take my business elsewhere sans any resolution. And it was probably better that way.

"We'll talk about this later?" May asked, looking for her notebook, anticipating the barrage of to-do's Stan would surely bark her way.

"Um . . . NO, we won't." I said and shuffled off, relieved not to be in her shoes as she headed into Stan's office. Walking down the hall and toward my office, I was also relieved to see Drew's door closed. I wasn't really up for a meet-and-greet. It was weird. We'd officially crossed the line and become friends the night before and seeing him this morning would have been awkward. (Especially after the way I'd left.) You know how it is when you kiss a guy friend, I mean really kiss him, and you see him the next day before either of you has had the chance to call the other one and break it all down in an *Okay, what was that all about?* way. That's how I was feeling. (I tend to analyze.) And no regrets, by the way. Trust me, I wanted this friendship. Drew was different from the friends I'd made thus far in NYC, and different is great, but I had woken up on a weird side of the bed and wasn't in the mood for anything out of the ordinary. I had gotten used to our subtle implications of mutual respect and camaraderie. I mean, as of today I knew about his sister, his college friends, the lackluster girlfriend. Was he now going to try to high-five me in the hallway? Would our friendship get people talking? 'Cause you know how people love to talk. Rather than get over-analytical—which I'm sure you could guess is something I tend to do and probably something I already had done where Drew was concerned—I made a beeline for my office, closed the door, switched on Howard Stern (yes, I admit it, I'm a fan), and savored that first great sip of coffee that usually helps put a cap-ital G in *Good morning.* I opened my window just a little to get some air circulating, kicked off my heels, flipped on my com-puter, and got straight to work.

Ahhh work—the ultimate distraction.

About an hour later I got an instant message from Drew:

Had a good time last night.
But says hi. How's Jake?
D.

Ahhh, the "call."

I smirked and, as I thought about when, how, if, and what I wanted to write back to him, I grabbed a chewed-up VIVIANLIVES engraved pencil that was sticking out of my overcrowded pen cup and tied my hair up in a knot. I also took a second to revel in the fact that my name was on a pencil. Then I grabbed my John Mayer CD and put it on. I'd had enough of Howard. (If we could only shut off every guy we found offensive.)

Smiling, I typed:

Leave me alone, I'm working . . . no buts! V.

And pressed SEND.
Two seconds later:

83

But . . .
D.

I decided to get up and go check in with Sheryl. (Momentary distractions in Web play curb the pace of anticipatory replies. Kinda like waiting two days before you return his call just because.) Drew had reached out first and, in my turn, I'd replied quickly. But I could feel shenanigans a-brewin' and I didn't want to get in over my head. Being his friend was evidently a bigger deal to me than I had thought, and to be honest my comfort level was a lot farther along than I would have otherwise imagined.

I could not figure out where the flirting line started and stopped. It was like playing with the morning's word game in the funnies section of the paper. You know what I mean, right? When the letters are all switched around? And at some point you just want to rip the paper apart and chuck it at someone. It took only minutes for me to think a million thoughts, see a million scenarios in my head. It was as if I had pushed FAST FORWARD on the VCR that is my mind and kept my finger on it. For a while.

Never mind.

Where was Sheryl? She was always great in the morning, totally fired up. Even after being awake since six A.M., having run what would register as half the island of Manhattan on some evil electronic exercise device. It was time to check in with her.

She was on the phone but invited me to come in and sit down anyway. She was talking a mile a minute on her headset. And simultaneously typing at her keyboard. She'd stop every few seconds to read a memo, file something in her desk drawer, and then go back to the typing thing. This went on for a little too long and was stressing me out. I signaled for her to *call me later* and went back to my office to hide.

My screensaver was already in effect. Omelet with a gold glittered tiara—in case you're interested. So if Drew had sent me another message, Omelet was now camouflaging it.

I decided to call Jack.

"Hell-o," he answered. His voice had a scratchy *I'm either hung over or still sleeping* sound to it. It was nice. He had worked a twenty-four-hour shift, and had probably gotten home by seven A.M. or so. It was nearly noon and I couldn't wait any longer. (I'm not allowed to call him at the station unless it's an emergency or something.)

"How are you, monkey?" I said. (That's my generic pet name for everyone I'm close to. I picked it up from my parents. The original "Monkeys.")

"Finnnne."

"You want to go back to bed?" I asked.

"In a minute. Howwww are you?"

"I'm fine. Go back to bed. I'll call you later."

"Come overrrr," he said. He sounded so cute I could eat him.

"After work, sweets. About seven."

"O-kaay. 'Night. Love you."

"You too. 'Bye."

I did love him ya know.

fifteen

Once a week Sophie and I met to get our nails, and whatever else needed fixing, done in Midtown. Her hours were godawful and well, let's face it, as the real world gets to become more and more of a reality and less and less of a saying, my best friend and I spend a lot of time apart. Respectfully, we always make sure to spend at least one evening together during the week and either a Saturday or Sunday, side by side, like the old days. And then, like I said, we rendezvous at "Nail Central Station."

I was desperate to see her. In the last twenty-four hours my emotions had gone into high alert, and although I had no intention of revealing any of them, her presence was always my remedy. So when I got her call, only minutes after hanging up with Jack, I was a very happy camper. I ducked out and got a cab lickety-split.

It was lunchtime and the city was groovin'. People everywhere with everything on their minds. Watching them is a favorite pastime for me so I was taken aback when I realized I was there. So quick! I stopped at the deli adjacent to the nail place and got Sophie her favorite: grilled cheese and tomato on whole wheat, with Fritos and a Sprite. I didn't hold back and ordered steak fries with gravy and a chocolate milk shake for myself. Bags in tow, I entered Nail Central Station only to find Sophie seated in the entryway, thumbing her two-way pager and looking more fabulous than ever. In an ivory floor-length coat with a groovy fox collar, unbuttoned and draped just so, revealing a black fitted turtleneck sweater, dark blue jeans, and brown pointy leather boots, I thought, *Hello S.Lo!* She had a big sloppy suede brown bag just next to her, filled to the brim with magazines and newspapers. And then there was her new b-day present from Ma and Pa, a sassy black and brass Balenciaga clutch bag, spoiled rotten since I can remember. I don't think my parents even know what a Balenciaga is. I mean, up until last year I would have thought Balenciaga was a small country in South America!

"Look at you!" I said and tossed her her lunch bag, which pissed her off momentarily 'cause she was in the middle of a "very important page."

"I know!" She laughed and gave me her signature Sophie smooch. "Oh good, you're using it"—pointing out the black Prada messenger bag I'd inherited from her a few weeks prior. (Don't ever be impressed by my accessories, by the way, as they're all basically hand-me-downs from her. Too bad we're not the same size!)

You could tell that she was so on her game. She was kicking ass at work; now an assistant market editor, she was officially doing what she loved. In one word, *shopping.* But not the way you and I do. Oh no. Sophie would travel from fashion house to fashion house, previewing collections before they shipped to stores, picking out the best of the best and handing them over to stylists and photographers to be photographed in magazines. She was even going to fashion shows. The girl was in heaven. Had she been in love, well, she'd basically be floating. But no such luck. Not yet anyway.

Our conversation began as it normally does, crunching on Fritos and french fries, her trying to convince me to get a "color" and getting frustrated when I insisted on "Like Linen." Soon after, she'd talk shop, literally, and I'd do my best to follow along. And it was all working. I was deep into catching up and critiquing. My drama was dissipating and I was relieved.

Sophie always takes longer, so she went first. Soon after, they were ready for me, so I sucked down a few more fries and headed over to the next available station. We were both equally bummed to find that we would not be seated together and made a point to exchange glances complete with lower-lip roll-overs that signified, *Oh no.* (Not being able to sit with a friend at a nail place is just like not being able to sit with your boyfriend on a plane, train, or automobile. Am I right?)

By my lonesome, I could only sit and stare at my nubby nails for so long. My thoughts began to surface, and I eventually got lost in contemplation. I knew that the problem I was having with Drew lay in the many problems I had had with Mark. Yup. Him again. I didn't have guy friends in college. I wasn't "allowed to," and honestly, at one point, it wasn't even worth the trouble any-more. And frankly, no one was really interested in the job if you know what I mean. Because it wasn't like he (Mark) was a closet freak show. Nope. He let the whole campus know that I was off limits. If someone even looked at me the wrong way, there'd be a threat of some sort. A scuffle at least. And that was just about the time I started staying home unless there was something that had to be done. Classes that couldn't be skipped, tests that had to be taken—that kind of thing. I withdrew from everything social because the likelihood of things getting out of hand was just too great. I was also very ashamed. I felt so defeated and I hated meeting the glances of anyone I knew. Somewhere along the way, I just got so tired. Tired of juggling his moods, tired of the fighting, and most of all too tired to do anything about it. And that's when it gets bad and you know you're in trouble. When you're trapped. Trapped inside yourself. Trapped in your own mind that's too weak to get you out of the mess you never signed up for. Why do women stay? I hate that question.

"Clear polish?"

"Nailtiques please."

It wasn't like guy friends were off limits in the beginning. No, no. At first it was more like, "Why go out with Richard or Mike when you can be with me?" Then came, "You know that Richard likes you, right? You know that he doesn't just think of you as a friend?" It wouldn't stop. "Right. Like you've never thought about Mike in that way?" and "You're wearing that to your study group? You want them to like you. Don't you?" It was incessant. "You probably tease them. You do, don't you? You want other guys to like you." I'd be lying if I sat here and said that I didn't at first think it cute—cute that my new boyfriend wanted me all to himself. No one had ever liked me like that before. But cute turned into scary before I ever knew what hit me.

Then and since, it was hard for me to get those questions out of my head. Difficult to understand how far was really too far when guy friends were concerned. And Mark was so good at twisting and spinning every detail, every response, every reaction, that for a while, a long while evidently, I thought that he might actually be right.

So with Drew I was divided. I felt guilty that perhaps, maybe, I did want him to like me. That I was being naive. That he didn't want to be my friend, but that he wanted to get down my pants.

That my attraction to him was "slutty," wanting him to want me, disrespecting Jack all the while. Did I? It was all so fucking confusing. Drew piqued my interest is all, right? *He seems like a cool guy and we work together, why shouldn't I want him for a friend?*

It was clear that despite the years and the distance, this fucking guy was still affecting me and I didn't know what to do about it but run, far and away from it. But Mark was long gone and I was still here. And with Jack and I doing well and Drew and I working practically door to door, I was screwed. Jack was becoming Mark in my confused subconscious, and Drew was turning into "them."

I moved over to the dryer and tried to talk to myself rationally. I needed to get Mark's voice out of my head. I quickly morphed old thoughts into new ones. A normal frame of mind. Jack was not Mark and a friendship with Drew was absolutely cool. Flirting was not a crime and surely, what I might have considered flirting would not exactly implicate me or, better still, make Drew think I liked him. Flirting to me, at this point anyway, was merely communicating with a cool person of the opposite sex. And that, my friends, had to change. I was young, I wasn't married, I'd done nothing wrong, and I was wasting brainpower on the biggest asswhole who ever lived!

Okay. I was back . . . if only for the afternoon.

Now let me find the quick-dry spray and get the hell out of here!

Sophie surprised me, needing to jet, without any polish even, as there was literally a "fashion emergency" to tend to.

"Go. Go," I said. "I'll call you later."

sixteen

By five-thirty I was famished, and although I knew that I'd be seeing Jack for dinner, I ran downstairs and over to the trusty street vendor who made the meanest shwarma pita pocket sandwiches. I know, this may sound vile, but I assure you, they smelled and tasted D-vine! And hands down worth the five bucks and the occasional stomach cramps they would leave behind.

About an hour later I adiosed the office. Careful to tidy up the place so I wouldn't have to come back to it a mess Monday morning. (Never a neat freak but always a big straighten-upper.) Drew and I left at about the same time, wishing each other a pleasant weekend, with not a high-five to be had. See, I had nothing to worry about.

I took the train straight to Jack's. He had called earlier, telling me not to worry about Omelet as he was on his way to my apartment to pick him up along with some of my things.

"What do you need? It's going to get cold this weekend."

"My cream-colored fisherman's sweater," I answered.

"And?"

"And, umm, I don't know. You pick some stuff out," I requested.

"Oh no. Then you'll have me to blame when you don't like your options."

"True." I chuckled. He was right about that. "Grab my jeans."

"Which ones?" he replied, frustrated.

"Whichever ones are on the floor." What? I'm sure, like me, you have more jeans than you can wear in a lifetime but the only ones you really ever do wear are the ones that only you think fit you so much better than the rest. The same ones that need washing but you rarely do wash them, 'cause if they shrink, well, it's all over. And these same jeans are usually the ones in a ball in the corner of your closets or slung over the nearest chair.

"And . . ."

"And some clean undies, a few white T-shirts, don't forget Omelet's food . . ."

"I won't."

"And bring my sneakers."

"Okay."

"We're not doing much this weekend, are we?" I asked, hoping that would indeed be the case.

"Well, Tom called. He and Lisa want to meet us for dinner."

"Can we do drinks maybe instead? I'm—"

Jack cut me off. He was very good about not creating a big thing out of me not wanting to hang out with his friends. "It's cool, Viv. Maybe I'll tell them to stop by my place later on. After they have dinner?"

"Oh my God, Jack. That would be so perfect." A chill night was so what I was in the mood for.

It was a cold evening and my black fingerless cashmere gloves were really becoming more victimlike than chic. Freezing and taxed from a long workweek, I was relieved to finally get to Jack's. I knew I was only a few floors away from being warm and cozy and loved. I looked up and could see Omelet standing just atop Jack's radiator, with his nose smushed to the window. (He has this endearing animal instinct. How he knew I was on the street below always blew my mind and broke my heart.) In seconds, Jack would notice the commotion and come to the window as well. There they were. Easily a J. Crew catalog photo op waiting to happen. Handsome and undone, there was my boyfriend and there was my Omelet, better than any teddy bear. It was moments like these when I felt more like a drama queen than anything else. When I could actually feel how lucky I was and could appreciate how good I had it.

One of my only regrets as a parent was not really ever taking the time to train Omelet. What was once a six-week-old eatable white puppy dog was now a one-hundred-pound colossal animal. He was too cute to discipline way back then. It felt cruel, even if he did eat one of my shoes or rip apart a handmade pillow. I was extra sensitive to commands, I guess, and felt that anything more than "sit" and "no" was a little demeaning. I know. I know. So now I was mom to an out-of-control lap dog who oozed affection and well, Omelet's "hellos" and "missed yous" were forces to be reckoned with.

Walking up the stairs, I was led by the delectable aroma of warm clean clothes, fresh from the dryer, and wondered if today was a special holiday that I had forgotten about. Jack hates doing laundry and usually gets me to do it for him with a clever bribe of some sort. I was happy to know that "housekeeper" would not be a hat I'd have to wear this weekend. Moments later and as I had expected, I was trampled by Omelet when I got to Jack's door. Jack and I could barely hug or exchange a brief kiss as Omelet was jumping and spinning and freaking out.

"Yes yes, hello baby. Hello. I missed you. Yes, I missed you. Awwwwww. Did you have a good day? Did you have a good day?" (I guess I thought if I repeated myself, Omelet would better understand what I meant?!?) After Omelet exhausted himself, I was able to take my coat off, undo my boots, stretch, and give Jack a big mushy greeting.

I so loved hugging him. I loved the way he smelled. Like shaving cream and baby powder mixed into one. I loved how hard he would hug me back. He was a bit of a mush himself. He followed me to his bedroom where I quickly changed out of the strict confines of my work clothes and into my sweater and sweats. On good days I'd think of Jack's apartment as a home away from home. There was Omelet right behind him, likewise waiting for some TLC. As I babbled on about whatever, giving up on my bra and just basically climbing out of it, Jack stood there, watching me instead of listening, sipping a cup of coffee.

Interrupted by my acknowledgment of his roaming eyes, he said, "You're beautiful. That's for sure."

Smiling, I asked, "Have you been listening to that Nelly Furtado record I left here?" Ha ha—not. He didn't get my joke and instead, rested his coffee on his dresser and tackled me to his bed.

Midair I farted by accident and it killed the moment, but at least now I had him laughing.

Shwarma!

seventeen

Whether it's a conscious move or not, just when things seem to be great with Jack, I always somehow find a way or a reason to push down a bit on the brakes. And it's only with hindsight that I realize I've done it.

See, things with my folks have never been perfect. There's always something going on in the Livingston household. Be it the highly problematic scenario with Simon and his wife, or—with my other brother Joseph—the fact that he's always trying to please our parents but then only ends up disappointing them 'cause he never delivers on near impossible promises. And then there's me, the "rebel," only because I'd opted to buck the female family tradition and actually try to do something with my life.

I think my mom and dad are frustrated is all. Just like we all do, they, too, probably had expectations and made assumptions. All three kids would stay close to home, marry someone they approved of, and live happily ever after. And, well, somewhere along the line, it didn't happen that way. And instead of embracing the brew that is us, it's like they pout and kick and scream on occasion. My mother especially.

It was on one such occasion, while I was spending the week-end with Mom as Dad was going out of town and she was all by her lonesome, that she pushed and pushed and pushed, as mothers often do, and, well, by the time I got back to the city, I was a head case.

The week after my cozy weekend with Jack, Omelet and I made the trip back to PA and got there on what became the latter side of Friday evening. Mom was never happier to see and spoil us, which, as you know, can be a wonderful, wonderful thing. She was in her trademark flannel long-sleeved nightgown, one of what is probably a collection of hundreds (all in one pastel color or another), with fluffy light blue slip-on slippers. Before Omelet went inside, he did his "lap," buzzing around and around my childhood home, which hardly thrilled my mom, as it had rained the day before and our backyard was one big mud pie that Omelet would soon bring in with him.

She held the squeaky porch door open for us both. With a heavy duffel bag over my shoulder and the rest of my stuff in hand I didn't have one free. It was good to be home. My house smelled like my house. She had been cooking up a storm, her vegetarian lasagna from what I could tell.

Putting my things away, in my room that had now basically become my father's study since I'd moved out, I hollered, "Smells great, Mom!"

"Jack mentioned how much he likes lasagna so I thought I'd send you home with . . ."

Signature Mom. Not five minutes inside and she was already planning my exit.

So, if I haven't told you already, she LOVED Jack. L-O-V-E-D him. I think the moment she heard that he was the fireman who'd rescued Omelet, she knew it was as close to a fairy tale as she'd ever be; now she was just waiting for "the call." She was in her late fifties and she had yet to plan a wedding for any of us, so you can't really blame her.

"Get down here, Vivian . . . let me fix you something to eat."

I changed into an old pair of college embossed sweats and a flowery cream flannel top. I stole a pair of thick ski socks from Joseph's room and slid on down the staircase and into the kitchen.

She was already feeding Omelet from the table, despite the instructions I'd been giving her for the last few years not to do that. But as "Grandma" she felt entitled to ignore them. Omelet has a very fussy stomach and I was pretty sure he'd mess the place by morning. *C'est la vie!*

Smoking her signature Parliament, she sat and stared at me while I ate. Tapping her foot, restless, eager to get on with "it." "It" being my answers to her barrage of questions:

1. Had I seen or spoken to Simon?
2. Had I seen photos of the baby?
3. Is Joseph seeing someone in particular?
4. Was there any truth to his comment about looking for work in Philadelphia?
5. Could I notice the difference in her forehead now that she was being Botoxed on a regular basis?
6. How were things with Jack?
7. Was I being friendly and polite where his family was concerned?

"Maaaaaaaaaaa!" I whined. "I'll be here all weekend. You don't need to ask me everything that's on your mind right this second!"

"Fine." She shook her head. "You're right."

I turned and gave Omelet a *Help me!* face.

"How are *you*, then, Vivi?" she asked.

I hated when she called me that. "I'm good, Ma. I'm good."

"That's good, dear."

"Yup." I was giving her a few seconds. A zebra never loses its stripes.

"So, hum, ah, well, have you seen Simon?" She blew the smoke to her right and stared at me all the while. My mom was like a wolf. All about the pack. All about loyalty. She was beautiful, with dark, dark hair. Still long enough to twist up in a ball like a ballerina, definitely not short like the rest of the women her age. She had creamy olive skin and huge brown almond-shaped eyes. She had a long smooth neck that propped her head up just so. And come to think of it, her skin really did look great. She was the kind of mother you didn't mess with when there was a curfew to be met. She was the kind of mom you wouldn't argue back at. She was a tough cookie in her pint-sized five-foot-two frame and growing up I either idolized or hated her.

Anyway, her last question came with a great deal of tension. My answer of course would be no, but I didn't feel like telling her so quickly. It pissed me off that she played this "thing" with my brother as though it were a game. If my dad, or Joseph, or I had even hinted at the fact that we wanted to see him, talk to him, anything, you could just tell she might actually out us right along with him. So in my own small way, fencing it for a few was retribution.

"Have you?" she questioned again, only this time she put her cigarette in the ashtray.

"*No*, Mom, I haven't okay . . . don't worry."

I could just tell that this was going to be a very long weekend and wondered if my dad was really away on business, thinking perhaps that he may have instead just simply escaped.

The phone rang and she got up to answer it. I wasn't moving. A home-cooked meal was a very hot commodity.

"Hi Jack!" she squealed in a schoolgirl-crush kinda way. (I told you she LOVED him.)

"How are you? Why didn't you come home with Vivi?"

Uch.

"Of course, those hours you keep. God bless you . . . Sure, here she is . . ."

"Vivian . . . it's Jack," she said, all smiles.

I took a deep breath, gathered my patience, and grabbed the phone.

"Hel-loooo," I said, as my mom overlooked.

"Hey babe. You sound funny." He laughed.

"Yeah well . . . ," I said.

"Go easy on her."

"Uh-huh. Can I call you later?" I asked.

"No, actually. I just got called in. I'm working through Sunday morning."

"Oh. That sucks. Will you try to call me then? If you get a second? Please!"

"Sure. Did you have a good drive up?" he asked.

"Yeah, easy."

"Good girl. All right, so I'll see you on Sunday night and I'll call you if I can."

"Okay, sweets."

" 'Bye, babe. Try to have fun. I love ya," he said.

"You too." I hung up.

Back at the kitchen table, she said it:

"When are you going to marry that boy?"

"Ma!"

"What, do you think he's going to sit around and wait forever?"

"I can't have this conversation again, Mom, I can't. Okay?"

The phone rang again, but this time it was her friend Vera and I was in the clear.

I watched her, watching me, seemingly delighted to have me home. Talking to her friend all blah, blah, blah. But her delight came in a very odd package. On one level I knew that she was happy. But there was this whole pent-up thing happening, too. Like, when something's about to fall. May not, but could. Do you know what I mean? If I was on my best behavior and told her exactly what she wanted to hear, then yeah, the weekend would be fine. But if I got real with her and got honest, she'd for sure send me packing and kick me right out. I was there as a substitute companion, a baby-sitter, an entertainer. I wasn't her friend.

And what's a girl to do? There's a time in everyone's life when you really get what you've got. You understand the dynamics and limitations of your family life and realize that testing the boundaries is too risky for the rewards that may or may not be waiting in the distance. And without my dad or Joe around to referee, I wasn't about to start playing.

As I was clearing and cleaning my dishes, she was just getting off the phone. I could hear Jack's words. Telling me to be patient. Reinforcing that this was, after all, "Mom." The queen of the household and I did love her gobs and I was resolved to be respectful and try my best to keep the peace.

"That was Vera," she said. "Her niece loves your Web site! My little Vivi."

Okay? My mom did/does not like what I do. Not for an instant. It makes her nervous and scared and I think she's afraid I'll get jaded. Or that somehow I'll fail and lose my wings. I think she knew that this site was just the beginning for me, the beginning insofar as it was the start of a personal and professional journey that wouldn't get me back, safe-n-sound in my hometown, anytime soon. Either way she rarely talked about it, so to me, that remark, however true, however genuine, was her peace offering.

I took Omelet out for a short walk and when I got back she had the television on in the den, with a very big threatening bowl of Doritos on the coffee table. "I thought we'd watch a movie!" she said when she heard me come in. "I got that one you like from Blockbuster . . . *Sixteen Candles*. I got some Sno-Caps, too!"

(Enter sound: *shake-shake!*)

Oh my. This was so cute and yet so tragic. I could just see her up there, paying for her Sno-Caps and a movie that probably hadn't been checked out for a decade.

But honestly, the fact that she remembered that I liked *Sixteen Candles* and that she'd made the effort at all, well, there was a brand-new optimism in the air. 'Cause at the end of the day, it's all about the little things that let us know they care. And for some strange reason those little things always seem to break through the minutiae of twenty-some years of baggage.

Why is that? Maybe 'cause those little things are just small gestures of a very big sentiment? Yeah, that sounds about right.

eighteen

The first part of the weekend flew. I slept in and soundly and it never felt better. There's always something real sweet and safe about nesting in my old room. (Even if it's been kidnapped by my dad's books and trinkets.) The dusty rose shag carpet is still as tacky as ever and my stuffed animals, although virtually abandoned, always welcome me with open arms. My cream-colored canopy bed still squeaks in all the same spots . . . charming in a very nostalgic way. Though I remember it being a real bitch on those random "late nights." The whole space seemed smaller as I got larger but other than that, it was all real good.

Somehow my mom talked me into going to her gym, better still, her aerobics class with the likes of Jane Fonda wanna-bes, leg warmers and all. My-oh-my. Rockin' to the oldies felt scary at one point, so I bailed and sipped orange juice at the snack bar in the hopes that this Saturday would soon pick up its pace. Afterward we hit the local strip mall. Jaded by NYC shopping, I just went along for the ride but was flooded with memories of Sophie and me. Remembering how this horseshoe of a shopping center had been our stomping grounds. Religiously spending our allowance there on one Pat-Benatar-esque item or another. Waiting for the shuttle bus that was our parents' station wagon to pick us up. Meeting up with boys behind the Burger King. Picking catfights and stare-downs with the girls from the Catholic school. Rocking our letter-man jackets in much the same way we now do our new handbags. Silly, silly, silly.

I remembered my shortsightedness. Never worrying or wondering about the world around me, focusing instead on homecoming and homework. Would the world ever feel that small again? I hoped so.

We had lunch at the diner, the same diner that I'd been to more times than I could count. But this time it, too, seemed almost miniature. Packed like an Easter Sunday, with young families and senior citizens, all making a big day of it.

"Sit up straight, Vivi . . . honestly, your posture is awful!" my mother barked.

Politely ignoring her, I asked, "What are you having?"

"I think just a small house salad and a cup of coffee . . . I'm watching my weight, you know."

"Yeah, like who isn't?" I murmured, holding up their menu, sized like a place mat, covered in coated plastic, filled with endless and basically needless pages of options. Props to Mom: I went with a Greek salad rather than the French toast and bacon special.

We both sipped away. Her, coffee. Me, iced tea. Funny. I noticed that she and I had the same exact hands and fingers. It was a very Discovery Channel moment, very *au naturel* but still kinda freaky. Her nails long, painted ruby red. Mine nice-n-nubby, in already chipping "Like Linen."

She noticed me noticing and said, "The exact same hands . . . and feet, too."

"How do you mean, Mom? Our feet?"

"Yup, Daddy used to always point them out to me. We both have a cute tiny small toe."

"Really?" I said. This was news. I went to check but I was wearing sneakers.

While still peeping under the table, I heard my mom shout, "Dani! Dani! Danielle . . . Oh look, Vivi, it's Danielle!"

Huh?

Before I could turn, there was Danielle, her husband, and a tiny little girl. Blond pigtails, big blue eyes, and some chocolate smudged over her pouty pink lips. Danielle and I were childhood friends who'd lost touch even before we went to college. She had gotten married just a few months after I first moved to NYC and, well, that was the last I'd heard from her.

"Vivian!" she said. "How are you?"

"I'm fine Dan, how are you? And who is this?"—pointing to her delicious daughter.

"This is Devon and my husband, Bill. You met at your going-away party, do you remember? Gosh, it seems like forever ago."

We all exchanged hellos and nice-to-meet-yous.

"I just love that Web site of yours. I go on every time I take Devon to the library. You're doing so well. You must be so proud, Mrs. Livingston."

"Very," my mom said as she made faces with Devon.

"So what have you been up to?" I asked as we all received *get-out-of-my-way* glances from the waitresses. We were filling up their lanes.

"Well, Bill and his brother just opened up a small restaurant in New Hope, so that's been keeping us real busy. And then of course, there's this little one (gesturing to Devon). She keeps me on my toes!"

"Wow. I bet!"

"Yeah," she continued as Bill put his arm around her, "and, well, we just found out, we're expecting our second. A boy this time!" She was delighted and her smiles were becoming contagious.

"Wow!" I said again. I didn't know what else to say. She was the only girl I knew who was my age who was going through all of this. "Wow!"

"Well, call me, Vivi, next time you're in town. We've got to get Devon over to her grandma's. Right, Dev?"

"Yup!" she said, clutching a naked Barbie with what looked like bed-head hair.

"Tell your mother we said hello," my mom said.

"Sure will, Mrs. Livingston. Great to see you, Vivi."

"Nice meeting you," Bill said as he picked up his daughter and led his wife through the restaurant.

Jesus, I thought, time to make this a Long Island. "Waitress!" I shouted.

They weren't even out of the diner before my mom tossed a Sweet'N Low at me and said, "See, Vivian. That could be you, too, you know."

"Mom!" I chucked the Sweet'N Low back at her. "Please don't start."

We both laughed, nervously.

"One day, Ma, one day," I assured her.

One day a VERY long time from now.

Check please!

Nineteen

Saturday night was short-n-sweet. Jack never did call and Mom had the girls over to play dominos aka mah-jongg so Omelet and I hid upstairs. I'd grown up in a household where TV was basically outlawed, and now, still without cable, well, I was thoroughly out of my element. Come to think of it, it was the same thing with junk food, another major enemy of the state, and well, a hell of a lotta good that had done me—not! My folks were big on reading, communicating, game playing. TV was "for idiots," my dad used to say. Suggesting coloring books over the likes of *Super Friends*. Ho-hum. And munchies and sweets: It was all bad. Cheerios replaced Froot Loops. Saltless pretzels instead of ice cream sandwiches. Growing up, my house was the one you probably skipped on Halloween. And I was the kid who got fired from every babysitting job 'cause I'd eat a family right out of their pantry!

So much for my father's ideology and my mother's guidelines. Right out the window once I started a life of my own. With hindsight, A.D.D., and a constant ten extra pounds, take it from me, ladies: It's all about balance I tell ya. A life without a middle ground is rebellion waiting to happen. Case in point: Subconsciously, I probably enjoy my *Sex and the City* over Cheez Doodles in a very different way from most of you.

Sorry for the tangent.

So, without a bevy of channels to surf, a bunch of friends to hang out with, or a boyfriend to complain to over the phone, I suited up and took Omelet for a midnight stroll. The air was cold and clean. The sound of hyperactive beetles and grasshoppers scared the shit out me at first, but I came to use them as my backup band after a short while.

As you'd probably expect, seeing Danielle and her Partridge Family fully freaked me out. I'd be lying if I said it had just felt like running into an old friend; it so didn't. I was happy for her, this is true. She just seemed so complete and satisfied, ya know. And it all just got me thinking . . . *What a lucky girl*. This cute kid, a devoted husband. It was beautiful. But to my mom's point, that, too, could be me, and I knew it. Jack was ready. Hell, my family was certainly ready. But alas, I was sure that I wasn't. And why was that?

Jack was everything any woman could want:

- Thoughtful
- Respectful
- Hardworking
- Kind
- Caring
- Devoted
- Hot!

What was I waiting for? What was it that I wanted? Of course I dreamed of being a bride. Being a mom. Building a home with someone. Making geometrically sliced sandwiches and stuffing them in brown paper bags. All that good stuff. But I did want a career. And in my mind, for some reason, I had to be single in order to get me one. I think it was because I wanted to come into that last important relationship on my own footing. Being good at something. Making my own money and having accomplished something.

It wasn't until Omelet stopped dead in his tracks and looked at me with this *How much longer will we have to walk until you feel better about yourself* expression that I realized how far we'd gone. I could see my grade school. It was right across the street. I remembered the playground and the small kickball field. The badminton birdie and the hopscotch flooring. It would be the perfect place for our own little version of recess.

So I let Omelet off the leash and we made our way past the parking lots and green sets of trees. Sure enough, everything was as I'd left it some fifteen years ago. Between the chunky stars and the bright lights of the school's courtyard, I could see and be seen just fine.

Safety first.

As Omelet familiarized himself with the area, I found a swing wide and strong enough for the likes of me. An accident waiting to happen. Rather than swing away, I decided to sway. I let my old boots glide back and forth through the dirt. They served as my kickstand. But I must admit, I was tempted to push myself off the ground and get closer to the sky. Higher and higher. Alas, I knew this swing would only be my rocking chair. 'Cause I could just visualize being found the morning after, suctioned to the ground by a rickety old swing set. Not exactly the way I wanted to be remembered.

Omelet came back, his fur newly decorated with a few pinecone remnants here and there, and found a comfy place just to my left to chill. Sprawled out but head up, he kept a careful eye on me and casually reacted to all the new sounds around him. He quite liked my playground, too.

Stuffed in and over a dark strip of rubber, from afar I must have looked like the Jolly Green Giant. And my current confusion began to feel incredibly apropos. I wasn't a kid anymore. I did need direction. There was a company relying on me, a perfectly nice guy believing that our relationship had meaning and purpose, and a little girl tucked deep within my interior clutching on to big dreams that needed filling.

I felt close. Close to accomplishments and close to a larger more profound understanding of myself. Beyond marketing and media, more and more I kinda knew that I wanted to be a writer. A novelist, maybe even a screenwriter. Something. And the Web site was furnishing me with the skills, confidence, and contacts to get there someday. I knew that. I felt as though I had lived a thousand lifetimes. I had hardly come full circle since college but I wanted to believe that I was on my way. I wanted to turn my experiences into chapters. Get girls thinking. Get them laughing. But I wasn't ready to admit it, verbally, that is. Not just yet. Quietly, I so enjoyed keeping my online journal. It kept me so connected to the world around me. I'd catch myself writing to the point where my own questions and dilemmas found explanations and answers. It was rewarding. It made me feel strong. It was my version of therapy.

That's what I wanted. I wanted to one day be a writer and feel a sense of calm. Find my niche. And I didn't think a guy could do that for me. I didn't think Jack could do that for me. Make me feel accomplished, whole, or satisfied and why should he anyway? Good relationships ground you, enhance you. I still felt broken and lost. I needed to find my own way before I could settle down. Imagine the responsibility of "fixing" someone while you're also supposed to be loving, honoring, and cherishing her? That's a lot of work.

Writing all these feelings down, thinking them and putting them in some kind of sequence that made sense, was one thing; expressing them was something else. I wished I'd been able to say all this to my mother when she'd nearly accosted me at our kitchen table the night before. But there was no way. She'd call me a "dreamer"; she'd think I was selfish. My mom knew nothing about my journey. And I didn't fault her for it, either. Having never expressed a shred of regret, not a single *what-if,* how would she ever get where I was coming from? She was Danielle and her life was everything she had wanted it to be. And if that all worked for them, that's great, but that's them.

That's why leaving PA was so important. Meeting new people, all equally screwed up or motivated or both. Had I not moved, started over, where would I be? Would I be Danielle? No. Because she was happy. I knew for sure that I would not have been. I needed closure and pride and Band-Aids. Lots of 'em. When I wasn't minding my kids or doing the dishes, I would have been reading magazines, going to movies, watching TV, or shopping Barnes & Noble always with a hint of regret. There would always be this mystery. Wanting to do something in addition to being a wife and mother but never knowing how, always thinking, *if.* And what kind of wife and mother would I be then? A fraud, a miserable fraud. I denied myself for four years in college and I'm still dealing with that shit to this day. Having learned from that big mistake, personal success was my option, settling was not.

That's why I loved New York as much as I did. It was a giant think tank. With images and people and opportunities in your face every day that make you feel and that are there to be seized. VH1 and Carolyn and Zack and seeing that other side of the world, the side I couldn't see from my view at Penn State, from my childhood bedroom window—that was when everything had shifted for me. When I realized that I could probably get away with a lot in this lifetime. At the very least, a derivative of an original wish. How many cities can offer you that? Fairy godmothers maybe, but cities, I don't think so.

It was getting late so I decided to head home. Omelet got up just as I did and I could tell he was ready for bed. Back on his leash and on our way home, our pace got swifter. Being in better spirits always does that to you. I had a slight butt cramp from the swing but that went away in good time.

It was a relief to be sure of myself. Sure that I was being true to my instincts and still fair to my dreams. Fulfilling them, or coming really close, would be my success. My own personal success, judged only by me. Because I'd tried. And that would make me happy.

Terrific. This all made great sense. But where did that leave Jack?

Not discussing my new mind-set with him would feel wrong. We'd been together for years. What if he was making normal assumptions about the progression of our relationship? What then? I knew I needed to talk to him when I got back to the city. I knew this because for the first time in my life, my reservations about our relationship were based not on fear but on truth and reason. And if he ended up receiving my revelations with approval and confessed that, like me, he was satisfied with the pace of where things were, then I'd just have my mother to blame. (Which wouldn't be a first. I assure you.)

As we rounded the corner of my block and cut through my neighbor's backyard, I once again let Omelet off the leash. Letting him get one good run in before we got back to NYC. It was then that I realized I'd left out a big fat *if*. What if Jack wasn't pleased with what I had to say? What if he wanted more?

Thought my plan was out of whack? That he belonged right up there while I lived my life to the fullest . . . what then? Was I ready for a breakup? Could I compromise? I didn't think so.

I got home and there was Mom, back at the kitchen table in another pastel nightgown. Smoking another Parliament, pretty, mysterious, and a little intimidating.

"Hey there, Vivi," she said.

"Hi Mom."

"Did ya have a nice walk?"

"Yeah, we went up to Woodgrove and back."

"That's some walk."

"Yeah, I'm beat."

"Do you know what time you're leaving yet? You wanna stay a bit longer and wait to see Dad?"

"Naaa, I don't think so. I want to leave early so that I don't hit too much traffic." I felt a little bad about leaving. I always do.

"That's okay, honey. I'll leave Jack's lasagna out so you don't forget it."

"Okay."

"Do you mind if I head on up to bed? I'm exhausted and I'm meeting Vera at seven. We're going to walk around the lake."

"No, that's fine. I'm tired, too."

"Okay, honey." She put her cigarette out and got up, carefully placing her coffee mug in the sink. "Have a safe ride home and wear your seat belt, okay?"

"Okay."

"Promise."

"Yes, I promise."

She leaned down and gave Omelet a kiss and a few pets good-bye. "You take good care of my Vivi, okay, Omelet?"

She gave me a hug and quick kiss on my cheek. "Good night baby."

"Good night Ma." I watched her walk out from the kitchen and up the staircase. "Send my love to Jack," she said midway.

"I will."

Her movements were a bit softer and slower than I had remembered and I got sad for a second. There was so much more we could have talked about if only we were different.

twenty

Curses. I had gotten back to the city, grabbed a change of clothes for work, a bit more food for Omelet, and schlepped all the way out to Brooklyn. Dragged my things, my dog, and that lasagna up five flights of stairs only to find a note from Jack. That he'd decided to spend the evening with his sister, mom, and niece Tatum, and he'd probably stay over: Tatum had her first ballet recital on Monday morning and he didn't want to miss it. He'd see me Tuesday morning.

Had he ever heard of a cell phone?

And the note went on . . . "I tried your cell a few times but I think you forgot to pay your bill again. I couldn't leave a message. Make yourself at home, J."

I rifled through my purse for my cell phone, eager to prove him wrong. But when I tried to call out I heard that dreaded . . . *ding, ding, ding . . . please contact so-and-so.*

My bad.

I decided to stick. It was late already and I'd found a great parking spot. I looked around and saw Jack's stuff everywhere.

Poor guy must have run in and run out. He was the greatest uncle, hands down. I put his clothes away, did his dishes, organized the clutter that was his coffee table, and poured myself a glass of wine. I searched and found the Norah Jones record I'd gotten him a few weeks prior, slipped it into his CD player, and tried to chill out. Having geared up for this grand conversation with my beau, I was anxious. Sitting there, I tried rehearsing with Omelet, role-playing if you will, but Omelet was way over me by then. We had already all but covered this on the drive home from PA.

I tried calling Soph to check in, but she didn't pick up. I rang May, who was M.I.A., as well. I was all about checking my voice mail but that wasn't an option. Which got me to reviewing my checkbook. Not a pretty sight. I poured myself a second glass of wine. I called my machine at home—no messages. Great, now I felt like a big loser. So I rationalized: My friends knew I was out of town, and besides I was sure I would have had an endless number of messages on my cell phone. Grrrrrrrr.

I stretched out, leaning my head back against the soft mushy cushions just as "Come Away with Me" began to play. Before I knew it I was startled by the deafening sounds of grouchy garbage trucks, hating their jobs just as much as you'd think they would. What? I'm sure they, too, had big dreams. Like a gig with Brinks or an ice cream man who'd take good care of them.

"What the devil . . ." I mumbled. It was bright outside and Omelet was nestled to my right. I looked at my watch and did a double take when I saw that it was almost six A.M. I took a deep breath and caught a glimpse of a photo of Jack and me. Uh-oh. It was now moonlighting as a coaster. I hoped Jack had made doubles.

The picture was a relatively new one that I hadn't remembered seeing before. It was at Madison Square Garden before or after a Dave Matthews show we'd seen together. Fun night. We had gone with Lisa and Tom, Dennis and Matt, and Jack's sister Gina and her boyfriend. Tom had won the tickets in a raffle or something and when we got the invite, it made an otherwise nondescript Tuesday night that much more exciting. And honestly, Dave does kill live. And Jack loves him in the way I do Madonna, so it was cool to see him so stoked. Beforehand we dined at The Independent down in Tribecea. Great steak au poivre and the most delicious watermelon martinis ever. Dennis used to date the bartender, so our drinks were on the house. (Which is always a very nice thing.)

I acknowledged my relief to finally be dating a guy whose friends I actually enjoyed being around. Yeesh, how much does it suck when we don't???

I got up and poked into Jack's bed nook. He wasn't in bed, though I wasn't surprised since he would have woken me if he'd come home. Must have slept over at his mom's after all. I took a nice long hot shower and shaved using Jack's razor. (Their razors are always so much better than ours.) It was early, and pretty nice outside, so I decided to go for a run along the waterfront and take in the city's skyline. From Dumbo, Jack's 'hood, you can see the entire Financial District and parts of South Street Seaport. It's also crazy 'cause you're practically underneath the Brooklyn Bridge. Yeah, that's right, I opted to exercise just minutes after I'd showered. Typical.

It was as if I had Brooklyn and Manhattan all to myself. No one but the garbage collectors and me were up at this ungodly hour. I quite liked it.

I've always had a love-hate relationship with exercise. I basically do it 'cause I have to, but on a few rare occasions I do find myself enjoying it. Like this morning for instance.

I'd never gotten into yoga and Pilates and all the other

regimes du jours that Sophie would take up after a courteous cue from one magazine or another. Nope. Not me. I was too anxious and stressed out to relax. I needed contact and movement, and running usually did that for me. Contact with the stones and pavement beneath my feet. The way I'd zone out— much like in a dark movie theater at that point when you focus in on the characters and the plot. Deep into the story, you block out the people, everyone, and everything around you. And then hopefully at the end you begin to come to, acknowledging the space around you. That usually happens for me when I run. I get into my head. I can hear myself breathing. I can feel my heart pumping and the way my limbs get heavier and heavier as I tire. I always feel as though I'm running away from something. Not in a cowardly way, but in a progressive one. I leave Mark behind, my work behind, my bills, my issues all behind. It's escapism at its healthiest.

twenty-one

Wouldn't you know it? The one morning when I was "running early" literally, the train I took into the city nearly derailed and I was stuck, along with what felt like a thousand other people, like sardines, panicked, anticipating a nasty spell of claustrophobia. And, well, I didn't get into work till almost eleven. And of course no one had a clue as to my whereabouts and, well, I don't need to get into it. We've all been there before.

When I arrived Sheryl was in my office and at my desk, searching through my Rolodex, looking for numbers upon numbers of friends and family, making sure I was in the city, somewhere, and on my way. Stan had actually left a Post-it note on my computer that ordered "See me." And Marni was shaking her head with sympathy.

"What?" I asked. "What'd I miss?"

Sheryl popped her head up and said, "Oh good. Good. Good. Good."

"Good what?"

"Good. You're here."

"You have no idea what hap—"

She cut me off.

"We don't have time to talk. Sorry. I got a call this morning from Jeanne Beker, of Fashion Television. She's in New York from Toronto and wants to interview you. This afternoon!"

"No way!" I said, completely astonished.

"Way," Marni said.

"Marni, grab my credit card. Get Vivian something decent to wear. We'll expense it. Call my friend Stella at Barney's, she'll help you. Her number's on my contact sheet."

Okay? What was wrong with what I had on?

Sheryl took a second to breathe and caught on to the fact that I was a wee bit offended.

"Get over yourself, Viv. It's an excuse for a new outfit. And it's on me."

That was true.

Quickly and happily, I peeped out my office door and called out to Marni, "I'm a size eight!"

She stopped, turned, and looked at me funny . . .

"Okay, a ten. I'm a size ten."

Back inside I said, "Um, Sheryl."

"Yeah."

"I've never spoken on camera before."

"You'll be great. You're on the Viv-cam every day," she said, basically ignoring me, focusing instead on finding our very best tearsheets of print spots we'd done before. My guess, they were for the piece for Fashion Television.

I didn't think it would make sense or help matters to tell her that I had always pretended that I *wasn't* on the Viv-cam every day, that I was hardly comfortable in front of a camera. Hell, I'm always the one who covers her bare arms or hides behind someone when those impromptu friendly photo sessions take place—shit! So, instead, still standing there in mild shock, I asked, "What did Stan say? Did you tell him?"

"Of course I did and he's thrilled." She then got all up in my "dance space," checked me out, and added, "Um, I think you should run around the corner and get a lip wax."

Youch. I placed my hand over my mouth and replied, "Oh. Okay."

I hadn't even taken my jacket off at that point so I grabbed my bag and made my way out and to the elevator.

"Hurry up, Viv," Sheryl shouted. "And leave your cell on. I'll call you in a minute and we'll go over everything."

Too embarrassed to tell her that that was an impossibility, I chickened out and said, "Will do."

Along the perimeter of the entryway, Stan was looking over something with Drew, May by his side. "Where are you off to?" he inquired. "You've got an interview here in just under two hours."

I put my hand over my mouth again and answered, "Just out. I'll be back in a second."

"What do you mean 'just out,' Vivian? You arrived late and now you're leaving? We all need to review what you're going to say, what you're not going to say."

"It's cool, Stan. I'll be back in fifteen minutes."

"It's school? What about school? What did you say?" He couldn't understand me.

"Uch! All right. I'm getting my lip waxed! There. Are you happy now? Sheryl thought it would be a good idea. So, um, I'll be back in a few minutes."

Drew tried not to laugh, but May couldn't be stopped.

Thankfully the elevator door opened and I jumped right in.

I stopped at a pay phone and called Sophie at the office.

She was going to flip. We'd both been watching Fashion Television, at her house—remember, I didn't have cable—since we'd hit puberty and this was, hands down, the biggest thing that had ever happened to me. My excitement was instinctual and thankfully, there wasn't enough time to be nervous about what would soon take place. Especially now that there were bigger fish to fry—i.e., apparently I looked like Tom Selleck.

And just as I had expected, Sophie thought I was putting her on. She cleared her schedule because she absolutely had to be there.

"Do you think Stan will mind?" she asked.

"Just wear something tight and preferably V-necked and he'll be fine."

"Done," she said. "I'm so happy for you, Viv! You're going to be great! Great!"

I gave her the vitals, asked her to call my parents, Joseph, and Jack, then hung up and headed straight to a nearby and very makeshift salon. There wasn't enough time for Nail Central Station. Which ended up being a huge mistake for reasons that I'm sure, regretfully, you can figure out all by your lonesome.

I got back to the office in record time but with a near third-degree burn on my upper lip. Lovely.

Stan was on eggshells. Probably because this morning, at least, he wanted to be on my good side. Which was something he found utterly uncomfortable. I inquired as to the substance behind the Post-it note and he said that we'd discuss it at a later date, which was totally fine with me.

While Marni was at Barney's, I noticed that May was rigging our conference room with beverages and hors d'oeuvres, some simple signage, and whatnot. She had some of the guys move the silverfish-gray sofa from the waiting area and place it in there, too. "Nice touch," I said and winked her way. When I got back to my office, where Sheryl had by now stationed the "Fashion Television Command Center," she introduced me to someone named Helena.

"Hi," I said. She was gorgeous in a very simple and very effortless way.

"Cheers," Helena said. "Great to meet you . . . please, have a seat." She had a British accent and in an instant I thought she was the coolest. I'd imagined that Drew's "But" looked a lot like her.

Anyway, Helena was a professional groomer whom Sheryl had called upon. She was to be touching up my hair and doing my makeup, which was a complete and utter first for me. And for a split second I felt like a movie star and it was awesome! *And*, she totally knew what she was doing, by the way. Soon my mouth only felt like it was on fire.

Before too long Marni was back, black garment bag in tow. Sheryl did the honors, opening up and approving her find.

"Stella said ivories would look good with Vivian's brown hair," Marni said nervously.

"I totally agree, Marni," Sheryl remarked. "Thank you."

"My pleasure," Marni replied ever-so-politely. "I'm going to see if May needs any help." This remark was phrased as a question, and as soon as Marni got a sense that it was okay with Sheryl, she was outta there. Something told me that working for Sheryl wasn't all rainbows and roses.

"So how did this all happen?" I asked over the roar of the blow dryer behind me. "Did Jeanne just call?"

"Please," Sheryl smugged. "I sent her a press kit a few weeks ago. Followed up and told her people that she'd have the 'world exclusive' if she wanted it."

"World exclusive?" I asked. It sounded so ridiculous.

"Yes, Vivian. This is your first-ever television interview. It was only a matter of time before producers started reading all our press coverage. Someone would have easily made this a TV story sooner or later. And, well, Jeanne checked out the site, and bingo. Even better, Fashion Television is also broadcast internationally, so women in Greece and Hong Kong, the Netherlands, pretty much everywhere will get a glimpse of you and hopefully start checking out the site."

She was good. Very good. Good at her job and even better at making me nervous! (Yeah, evidently, there was enough time.)

Oh my . . .

I changed into this beautiful white jacket that zipped up the front and had poufed-out shoulders and long exaggerated bell sleeves. It fit perfectly and was so going to be a keeper. Next were the pants, and I was very hesitant about trying them on. Imagine the horror of them not fitting? They were low-waisted, boot-cut chino corduroy trousers. They were so soft and they fit me perfectly, which was a HUGE relief. They were a bit long but because I'd be seated, Helena and Sheryl agreed that it wouldn't be the end of the world. Thank heavens. I was to be wearing Sheryl's brown boots but when we figured out that she was two sizes smaller than me, I knew who to call: yup, Super-Sophie!

She ended up bringing three brand-new options from her fashion closet at work. None that I could keep unfortunately, but all equally fabulous. I let Sheryl do the honors. She chose a strappy pair of Jimmy Choos and my piggies were pleasantly pleased.

Before too long Helena was finished and decided to check out the lighting in the area in which I'd be filmed. Stan entered and Drew followed, so Sophie scrammed and together we four shut the door and got serious. Did we know what questions would be asked? Was I to be answering technical questions? Make references to traffic and ad rates? What if I cursed? It was all a bit overwhelming and every fiber in my body wanted to call Mom.

Interesting.

Stan started really freaking me out. Try as he may, his concerns and criticisms were not coming off as suggestions and my stomach started acting up. Which was followed by hot flashes and so I began to unzip my new jacket-blazer thingy. That was until I saw Drew's face and realized that, having gone a bit over-budget, Stella and Marni had not packed a shirt!

Sheryl saw my strip tease, too, and we all started laughing, all but Stan, which semi-eased the tension.

Drew attempted to get it together and just came out with an, "I think we should let Vivian say and do whatever feels right to her."

I was shocked.

He went on, "She's been on the other side a hundred times before."

Sheryl and Stan said nothing.

"Am I right, Vivian . . . at VH-One???" Talk about "leading a witness." Drew was nudging me to stand up for myself and without many options, I took his cue.

"But she has no formal media training?" Stan whined while looking at Sheryl, suggesting her mistake in overlooking what he felt to be critical criteria. If she were to be pitching me for television, she should have simultaneously been booking me some training time.

Sheryl was speechless and I quickly came to her defense, getting the conversation back on track. "Yes Drew. I'm pretty sure I can do it. I know what will make you guys happy and what wouldn't. It'll be fine." I was completely full of it. Or was I? Either way I deserved an Academy Award nomination. My stomach had more butterflies than Mariah Carey has on her clothes, on her albums, or in her apartment. And it was also pretty safe to say that I had two enormous sweat stains under each arm. Grace under fire—hardly!

Sheryl and Stan exchanged glances and shrugs while Drew and I looked at each other, determined and a little scared.

It was decided. I'd be winging it.

Ladies, start your engines!!!

twenty-two

Suffice it to say, I survived. Sure, it could have gone better, but you know what? It could have gone a lot worse, too. Better still, everyone, including Stan, seemed pleased. Sheryl was actually beyond pleased. She thought it was fantastic, but you didn't have to be a genius to know that after Stan's formalized faux paus, that whole "media training" thing, she had no choice but to shout "Well done" loud and proud if only for the sake of her own employment. 'Cause that's how bent out of shape Stan was. And you know what, you'd better sit down for this one, I semi sort of agreed with him. Sheryl had put the cart before the horse with this one, but I guess sometimes you need to do that to make things happen. Especially where public relations is concerned. If you snooze you lose. So instead, you wake right up and cross your fingers.

But let's focus on the fun stuff, shall we?

I powwowed with Sophie and May in the bathroom only seconds before we were set to tape. Looking out the window, I cautiously calculated the distance between my position and the ground. How much harm I'd really cause myself if I elected to jump. So they sat me down, on a toilet for lack of a more comfortable alternative, and huddled around to do their best to calm me down.

"Try to pretend that she's your friend. Like she's me," Sophie said. "And how comfortable are you talking to me?"

"And really, Viv, who better than you to talk about what we do? You and I both know that you can talk on and on and on about this site, this business. C'mon Vivian, you can do this with your eyes closed. Seriously," May insisted.

Then Sophie added something like, ". . . and you look amazing! Think of how many millions of people are going to see you and how . . ." And then May stepped on her foot, thinking that I didn't see her do it but I did. So she regretfully retracted, "Okay, you don't really need to be thinking about that right now."

Sheryl barged in and said, "Okay, baby. You ready?"

"No." I stood up.

She signaled for May and Soph to move aside. She grabbed my hand and coaxed me out of the stall. Then she came around and stood behind me. Gently nudging me forward. "Sure you are. You're going to be great. We all believe in you. It's just the first of many interviews to come!"

"Vive Vivian!" Sophie shrieked, which made me laugh and got me embarrassed but was just so pure and sweet that I took her joy with me and went out there—slowly.

It was just like in the movies. Lights, cameras, cameramen, Helena with blush brush in hand, Stan seated alongside Drew at the head of the conference table, behind the crew. I could see two of the three witches of work-wick peering in from outside, which in a spiteful kind of way made it clear I'd have to kick some serious ass in this interview. It wasn't paranoia but more like instinct that told me they'd dance around some random bonfire, shrieking and hissing, if I made a colossal mistake.

Sophie was standing next to May and Helena. Marni was sipping her soda, nervously, out of the can. From what I could tell, the can never left her lips. It was as though she was too focused on what was going on to remove it. Like a pacifier. Sheryl was standing over Stan, hugging a clipboard with one hand, giving me a courtside thumbs-up with the other.

Two guys sat me down and miked me and Jeanne came over and introduced herself. I was careful to maintain eye contact with her. It was something that I'd picked up from Carolyn at VH1. Whenever she was in conversation with someone whom she was either interested in or intimidated by, she always balanced his or her glance. It made her seem powerful, interested, respectful, and on the same playing field. I'd never forgotten that and I hoped it would work for me now, too.

I could feel and basically hear my knees knocking as Jeanne exchanged small talk with me in an obvious and kind attempt to make me feel at ease. It half worked.

Long story short, Jeanne Beker was brilliant. She was funny and smart and professional and very understanding of my stage fright. She had done her research and I could barely contain myself. Every time she referred to the Web site, to our clients, to journal entries I had written, I must have had this *I can't believe you know about that?* kind of look on my face. I was floored. (Being flattered throughout an entire interview can sort of downplay your property if you know what I mean.) Anyway, she knew all about the site and asked a lot of great questions. She even asked me about my family and about Omelet and about Jack!

I kept the pep talk that Sophie and May and Sheryl had given me close to my heart as I did my best to be myself while also coming off professionally and articulately. I had seen Jeanne interview all the greats and it was beyond surreal to be sitting there, chatting with her. So much so that throughout most of our conversation, I was sure I'd been dreaming.

So yeah, I did it and the segment aired some two weeks later.

Can you even believe?

twenty-three

ooking back, those two weeks prior to the debut of my interview on Fashion Television were kinda like the calm before the storm. On every level. It was as if our entire little company was both impassioned and terrified of what would be our future once the viewing public got a real whiff of me.

Sheryl, the consummate overachieving neurotic told-you-so PR queen, did everything in her power to position the interview as "just the beginning" of phase-two-type goals and initiatives of the company. Because Forever After, Inc., had never shot an ad campaign, had never solicited its user base, she and basically everyone else felt that this exposure would either open or close many a door—nothing like a little pressure, eh?

An electronic memorandum went out to all staff members that absolutely no new business, other than creative content for the Web site, should be conducted until after the airing. The company was looking for a reason to up its advertising rates and felt that Jeanne's interest and endorsement of both myself and the site might be just the way to do it. Unbeknownst to me (at least until May overheard a conversation between Stan and Drew and the other powers-that-be in his office and subsequently filled me in), company execs were also hoping that licensing opportunities would start to trickle in. That maybe, just maybe, a creative business-minded person would tune in, experience the interview, and finally "get it." Get that we were bankable, as in "not going anywhere," as in not giving up and throwing in the towel because we'd never become the portal that we'd never even wanted to be but everyone assumed we should. Get that we were original; that our voice, what we stood for, from our business model to our content, was clever, pioneering, and honest. And finally, get that vivianlives.com was indeed slowly becoming the virtual home-away-from-home cyberhangout for women that we'd always wanted it to be. A novelty with loads of potential. And, well, if we could achieve that, maybe there were other things out there for us.

It all sounded plausible in theory. That is, without factoring in a difficult economy and the horrific reputation that shadowed everything "Net" of late. But I was an optimist. At least I tried to be and, well, we'll just see, I guess.

Anyway, during this same time Sophie was out of town, shooting on Shelter Island—a beautiful spot in the Hamptons. May's sister had broken her leg, having slipped after heavy rain in the lobby of her building, so May was baby-sitting a lot. And Jack was forever at work or on call, so keeping busy, trying to take my mind off what was the "Fashion Television Countdown," was as arduous as you could imagine. And my family members were of no use. They "knew" it would be brilliant.

So more often than not, Drew and I found ourselves at Luvas, taking the collective edge off. Sure, his work was done behind the camera and if the interview tanked, he'd pretty much be no worse for wear, but he did take the time to remind me that, professionally, this was a very big deal for him. He noted that Stan would forever hold him responsible if it didn't go well. After all, it was Drew who'd cheered for me, easing Stan into the idea of my abilities. Which was a good point . . .

Bartender!

Huddled in what was slowly becoming "our corner" in the front part of the bar, Drew and I swapped stories and anecdotes, celebrity crushes (Brad Pitt and Cindy Crawford, respectively), regrets, personal insecurities (my body, his bank account). Then after we had both successfully but momentarily tossed our interview jitters aside, one of us would always revert to business. Tonight it was his turn:

"I think finally putting a face and personality to the name— nationally, that is—was the best and probably the only thing we could have done. Sheryl's right, Vivian, it would have happened sooner or later and the fact that she pitched it and booked it and approved it with enough time to properly position it, well, hats off to her!"

"She's a good one to have on our side," I added.

"Absolutely," he agreed and raised his shot glass, inviting me to do the same.

"Eww, Drew. Tequila? Really? Is this that necessary? Just the smell of it is bringing me back to a very bad night in Cancún!"

"You're a tough one, Vivian. I'm sure you can handle it. Now then . . . to Sheryl!"

"To Sheryl" I repeated, raised my glass, and clicked his, a little hard actually, hoping that a nice bit of my tequila would spill out, but it didn't.

Gulp.

Uchhhhhhhhhh.

He searched for his cigarettes while I chased the shot with a by-now-lukewarm Amstel Light.

I heard my cell phone ring but by the time I found it, I'd missed the call. (Yeah, my service had finally been restored.)

Lighting up, Drew could see my displeasure. "Gimme a break, Viv. I'm under a lot of pressure. Have you ever smoked a cigarette?"

"Actually, I haven't," I replied proudly. It was one of my more interesting stats. (I don't have any molars either, no wisdom teeth, nothing—but let me go on.)

Surprised, he asked, "Never?"

"Nope."

"Hmmm. Well good for you, it's a gross habit." He puffed away.

"Yeah, it is actually. But if you really want to know, there was a point in school where I wanted to. Just to see what all the fuss was about."

"So why didn't you?"

" 'Cause I thought I'd like it and would never be able to quit. Willpower has never been my strong suit."

"Yeah, I hear that." Puff. Puff.

Before I could dive into that remark, our waitress dropped off another three sets of tequila shots. I took a deep breath, not sure if I had the capacity to keep up with Frat-Boy Drew here. Questioning, too, what good it would do me to get drunk and, furthermore, get sick by the time I got home, if I was lucky, and spend the wee hours of the morning on my bathroom floor.

So we did another and, for whatever the reason, I just had to ask . . .

"Okay, Drew. I have to ask you something and I want you to give me a straight answer. Okay?"

"Okay?" he said, visibly struck with curiosity.

"Is your name really Andrew?" After a slight pause, I made a funny surprised-type face and raised my eyebrows, willing the truth.

"Noooooo." He chuckled. Unconvincingly, I might add. "What kind of question is that?" Then he shifted around in his seat.

So I pushed. "Are you being honest with me . . . Drew?"

I was certain by that point. 'Cause he was totally aghast—not with shock as in *What could she be thinking?* but more like, *How did she find out?*—and as women we often know when we're being lied to. Especially if we're not sleeping with the guy who's doing the fibbing.

He signaled that he would give me a straight answer if I did another shot. I told him I'd only do another one if he answered me.

"All right, all right . . . you got me. BUT, I changed it legally once I graduated college."

"I knew it!" I screamed with delight. "I knew it!"

ANDrew was able to laugh at himself, too, which pretty much canceled out how girly, narcissistic, and lame I thought he was at that moment.

Just then, his cell phone rang.

Relieved, he said "Saved" and without a purse to search through, he picked up his phone in time enough from the small end table next to his chair.

I assumed it was "But," and with enough experience with Drew to know that their phone calls were usually long-winded and tempestuous, I decided to find another photo on Luvas's wall to keep my attention.

This time it was a woman, tanned and in a seventies hipster bikini, about to jump into the arms of her man, who was in an oval, stone-lined in-ground swimming pool, water up to his waist, arms up, out and ready to catch her. He was on the skinny side, rather pale, and his hair was still dry and in desperate need of a cut. He had scruffy sensational sideburns that balanced out his longer-than-average nose.

Hmmmmmmm. What was their story?

But there was no time to hypothesize. Drew clicked his cell phone shut and stared my way. He told me to raise my shot glass, as he did his.

"No, no. Not yet," I urged. "I need to put some distance be-tween these things."

"That was Sheryl," he said. "The interview got pushed up a week and it's airing tomorrow night."

"No." I panicked. "No. It's not."

"Yes." He smiled.

"Oh God."

Never had fear materialized within my body in such a way. Like a tranquil airplane flight that's suddenly interrupted by tur-bulence, and afterward you basically need to pick your heart up off the floor and glue it back together. It kinda felt like that.

"Are you okay, Viv?" Drew asked nervously. "You look a little sick."

"Ummmm, I don't know," I murmured. And I didn't. Was I about to throw up? Flip out? Or laugh my ass off? It could have gone any way really.

Drew raised his shot glass, as did I . . .

I started to giggle and then my giggle turned into a laugh and then my laugh turned into a cackle. The likes of which I'd never heard come from my body before.

"To you, girl. You take fuckin' chances and I love that about you! To whatever happens!"

What was happening? Was I mad?

I was literally and figuratively out of control. It was as if I was some wild virgin bungee jumper who instead of crying or whimpering with regret, just seconds before blastoff, chooses to bask in the craziness of it all, shouting and woo-hoo-ing.

A brand-new instinctual reaction I guess, that I'd never seen coming.

We threw another shot back, which made me burp. Which, of course, was pretty embarrassing but only made me laugh more. It was as though I had hijacked my nervousness and much to my surprise was turning it into a celebratory, fuck-it kind of excitement. I started laughing again, my eyes closed, the tequila slowly showing me who was boss.

Suddenly, time seemed to stop. Almost skipping as I felt a cold hand cradling my jaw and cheek. Barely moving, almost resting there, very gently. Gingerly. Sweetly. It postponed my first impatient rational thoughts, so I kept my eyes closed for another moment. My mouth nearly shut, I could feel a cold air seeping through the small space of my two lips. Making them dry. Making them stiff. In what amounted to a mini second, I realized what was going on and I opened my eyes, but by that time I could only see the outline of Drew's face. The stubble on his cheeks, so close up they looked more like polka dots. I stayed still and a slow easy questioning kiss locked my lips. I could taste the strange mix of tobacco and tequila on Drew. Even more, I could feel the impulsive nature of it all.

The kiss took on a life of its own. Both of us, I think, scared to open our eyes and lean back and away from the other. And so spontaneous that toward the end it, too, came with a hint of caution and regret.

I placed my hand on Drew's knee. I could feel the small spaces between the lines of his corduroy pants. I pushed down and broke away. Needing to do something, I used the same hand to wipe the corner of my mouth, almost in slow motion, hoping that he would say something in between. It was hard to look his way, but I did.

"Should I apologize?" he asked.

"I don't know," I said.

And I didn't. I wasn't mad.

"Will you excuse me, I'm going to go to the ladies' room."

"Sure." He stood up, as did I.

I grabbed my purse and made my way to the back of the bar. The place was packed and the usually short distance felt more like a walk than a quick trip to the loo. So dark, you could barely make out the person in front of you. As I maneuvered my way between bodies and shifting forms, to be honest, I was both delighted and horrified. Shocked really. Blown away by his bold move. Plagued by my obvious reciprocation. I hoped there'd be a nice long line that'd give me enough time to figure out what had just happened and, more importantly, why. And I knew better than to blame it on a few shots and a warm beer.

"This Kiss" by Faith Hill reared its head from the speakers. What timing.

Lo and behold, as I had wished and half expected, the line for the bathroom was enormous and stretched out like a centipede around the back of the bar. We were like an endless row of fully clothed cheerleaders, observing and ready to root for the teams of male pool players who were fixated not on us, but on their games.

Minutes multiplied and the line wasn't moving and I had more than enough time to toss and turn over Drew. Before long I'd positioned the kiss as a very impromptu moment. It really was the ideal time for a kiss; more ideal of course if I didn't have a boyfriend or Drew a girlfriend, but what was done was done.

But it was a pretty great kiss.

But it was a moment is all.

A great moment.

Fuck!

I was taken aback, way aback, when from behind I felt a hand on either side of my waist. *Is he crazy?* I thought to myself. Following me to the bathroom and groping me in public was completely inappropriate. Or perhaps, better put, more inappropriate than . . . But before I could turn around to shoo him, my right ear was kissed. And that was enough!

"Stop it Dre—"

"It's me baby—take it easy!"

I turned and there was Jack.

"Hi," I said. "You scared me."

"Sorry, sweets. Sneaking up on you in a place like this probably isn't the best idea."

"No, no it's not," I said.

"How long have you been here?" he asked.

"Oh, just a little while."

"Where are you sitting?"

"To the right of the doorway."

"I must have missed you. I got here a few minutes ago. I'm with Matt. Dennis is meeting us. We have a while to go before we're up." He gestured to the pool table on the far right.

"Oh," I said.

"You here with May?" he said. "Where's that kid, she's always telling me she can take me in pool. I'd like to see her try."

"Yeah," I said.

He leaned in and kissed me.

"Somebody's been drinking . . ." he laughed.

"Not really." I tried to put some distance between our bodies. My conscience was taking up too much space.

"You're better off . . . going back up to your office," he said.

"Huh?"

"To pee. This line ain't moving."

"Okay. Yes, you're right. So I'll see ya later?"

I turned and tried to make a break for it but he grabbed the belt loop on the back of my pants and put me in reverse.

"Where are you going?" he asked flirtatiously. "Looks like someone's a little out of it?"

"Oh, yeah, I am. I'm sorry."

"You want me to get you a cab? Do you need me to take you home?" he said.

"No. No I'm fine. You play your game. I'm gonna get going. Call me later?"

"Sure," he said. "You want me to come over? I got word this afternoon—I'm off for the next forty-eight hours so I can sleep over if you want."

"Sure," I said.

I gave him a quick smooch and began to walk away. Once I was sure I'd blended in with the crowd, I bolted.

When I returned, Drew looked as if he'd sobered up.

"I thought you'd escaped out the back door," he said. "I got us a few glasses of water. Here."

"I have to go," I said, picking up my coat.

"What? Wait. Why?"

"I just have to go."

He grabbed my wrist and apologized. "Vivian, listen, I'm sorry. There's no need to leave."

Confused, freaked out beyond words, and a little fucked up, it was hard for me to juggle the realities that were hitting me from every angle but before I could explain, I heard Jack call my name.

"Vivian!"

I turned and saw him standing there with Matt. And there I was, frazzled with a strange guy holding my wrist.

"Hi." I smiled.

"Hey," Jack said.

"Hi Matt," I said.

They both were staring at Drew.

"Hey," Drew said, placing his hands in his pockets.

"You guys," I said, walking toward them, then grabbing Jack's hand and pulling him toward Drew. "This is Drew. Andrew really. Wait. Forget it. Just Drew. This is Drew. We work together."

"What's up man," Jack said flatly. I couldn't get a good enough read on what Jack's tone of voice meant, if anything. It was too noisy and too dark to pick up any subtle facial expressions.

"Nice to meet you," Drew said with arm outstretched, hoping to shake Jack's hand. "Vivian's told me a lot about you."

"Yeah?" Jack shook his hand.

Drew and Matt exchanged quick pleasantries.

"So I thought you were here with May?" Jack said.

Great. Enter big fat lie: "She was here but then she left. 'Member I told you about her sister . . ."

"Oh yeah, how's she doing?"

"Who?" I asked.

"May's sister."

"She's fine."

"Hey," Drew said. "I'm gonna get going. Viv—I'll see ya tomorrow. Jake—great meeting you."

"Jack." Me, Jack, and Matt all said it at the same time.

"Sure, of course. I'm sorry—it's the tequila. All right then . . . have a good night." Drew left the bar in a split second.

Matt excused himself and told Jack he'd meet him back by the pool tables. "Later Viv," he said to me.

"Later Matt," I said.

"What the hell is going on, Vivian?" Jack looked more hurt than angry.

"Nothing," I urged. "Nothing. What do you mean?"

"What did I interrupt?"

"Nothing."

"Do you think I'm an idiot?"

"No. Of course not."

"Then tell me what was going on?"

"Jack—nothing. Nothing was going on. You're being crazy. Drew's my friend. We work together. I just came back after seeing you and I told him that I didn't feel great and that I was going to leave. He just wanted to make sure I was okay. Honest. That's it."

"Really?" he asked.

"Of course."

He hugged me and whispered in my ear, "I love you, babe. Sorry. It just freaked me out for a second."

"Shhhh," I said.

I felt terrible.

He kissed me on my cheek and walked me outside to get a cab. "I'll be another hour. I gotta stick around until Dennis shows up. Then I'll come over."

"Okay," I said.

I kissed him good-bye and once I got a cab, he went back into the bar. I felt sick. A mix of guilt and alcohol did me in and, sure enough, once I got home it was all about the bathroom.

When I woke up the next morning, Jack was passed out beside me. And for a moment it was another normal morning. But a second after that, I knew that everything had changed.

twenty-four

On my way to work, sipping my coffee, I began to come undone. I could have schmeared the pressure I was feeling on my bagel! And unlike the night before, this morning, laughter was not my best medicine. When I thought about the day ahead, I wanted only to close my eyes, lie on the floor of my office, and (like my beloved heroine Snow White) wait for Prince Charming (who would be wearing that costume was not very clear) to kiss me and tell me how it all went down.

Screw all this memory making; wake me when it's over!

I dodged just about everyone and breathed a sigh of relief when I shut my office door behind me. Besides the frenzy of the pending Fashion Television interview, I was also not ready to deal with Drew—I was so ashamed of my behavior. I kept recalling the events that had led up to the kiss. Had I somehow invited it? Mark's voice quickly came into my head. All his harsh words and accusations. Was he right about me?

I had been on the receiving end so many times, and there

was nothing worse. And I'd never thought I was capable of doing that to someone I cared about. Sure it was just a kiss, but for me a kiss can be more intimate and more meaningful than its brevity suggests. Worst-case scenario, I'd rather Jack romp around on the beach with a meaningless stranger than be swept away by a smooch. Sounds crazy but it's true. But enough of this hypothetical, just visualizing it was making me uncomfortable.

I drew the blinds, flipped on my computer and lit a candle, having never turned on the lights. I searched for something calming to listen to and thought that a little Stevie Nicks might do the trick.

I found it difficult to do much of anything, though. My fingers were too jittery to type. My palms too sweaty to file. My conscience too heavy to phone my friends. That Post-it from Stan was still clinging to my monitor, so I elected to buzz him and see what he wanted.

May picked up his phone and, naturally, talked about the TV segment.

"Stan wants to order in a bunch of pizzas and have everyone watch it together in the conference room tonight . . . you in?" she asked.

I didn't know how to respond.

"Pepperoni and sausage pizza . . ." she bribed.

"Um. I don't think so. You guys should all do it. But the thought of being in the same room with everyone, at that moment, feels unbearable," I said, semidistracted, playing with the sticky old Post-it note in my hand. It had a wiry long hair stuck to the back of it, most likely one of mine, that refused to come off. I crushed it and chucked it . . . ten points!

"I don't think Stan will take no for an answer on this one, Viv," she said.

"Well, he might have to May, ya know?" I quipped.

"You should try to get into this, Vivian. How often does something like this ever happen to someone?"

"You're right and I know, but I'm just not sure yet, okay? I'll have to see."

"Okay," she said.

"Can I talk to Stan? Is he there?"

"Sure. Hang on a second."

Soon after, his voice came on the line. "Hi Vivian."

"Hey," I said. "So, the Post-it note. Whatever happened with that?"

"Oh sure . . . (clears throat) I want you to start thinking about music."

"How so?" I asked not knowing where he was going. "Selling it, endorsing it, making it?"

"No, not making it," he said, laughing. "I've heard you sing . . ."

"When?" I laughed, too.

"Remember our holiday party last year and the karaoke machine . . ."

"Enough said." Yeesh, I sure did.

"Right, so I have a friend who's in the business. His name's Hawk."

"As in mo?"

"It's a nickname, Vivian. Anyway, he checked out our site and was intrigued. Thought there was opportunity for a music component. A stronger presence. I thought I'd get you and Drew and him in a room. He'll be in New York next week. So just give it some thought. Powwow with Drew. The two of you always come up with great ideas."

It was unlike Stan to be this nice and encouraging.

"All right," I said.

"We'll be seeing you tonight? Seven o'clock?" he asked.

"Maybe," I said. "Not too sure I want to watch it. Especially with everyone around."

"Well, you think it over then . . . You should ask your friend Sophie to join us."

Ew, ew, ew. "Okay."

"Bye-bye."

"Bye."

Music. That would be cool. Maybe a countdown. Maybe Q&A's with musicians. Hmmm. Maybe a mixed tape! How much do we love those but who has the time or the new know-how required to make them anymore . . .

We should do records! I thought. A themed mixed tape kinda thing. I could pick the greatest songs to work out to, drive to, dance to, chill to, and even kiss to. (Ha, ha, ha.)

There was a knock at my door and I asked, "Who is it?" in a very little red riding hood kinda way.

"It's me," I heard.

"Me who?" I asked, buying time and sort of hoping it was Sean, the tech support stud I'd e-mailed a few days prior, to help me with my laser printer.

"It's Drew . . . can I come in?"

I quickly blew out the candle to keep from looking like a freak. It was not even noon and I was burning in the dark. Fussy, the wick wouldn't quit, and I found myself hunched over it, like a schoolgirl without enough breath to blow out the seven pink candles mounted atop a homemade birthday cake.

"Viv?"

I'd forgotten to answer him and said "Sure," staging a World Series game face. Just as he opened the door, the candle went out and my office went dark. With Stevie in the background, well, you can certainly surmise that my chill-clad work environment read *peculiar* at best.

"Do you mind if I turn on a light?" he asked hesitantly.

"No, please do." I chuckled.

He was careful to leave my door open a pinch and then looked over my head and on to the still-curious but now half-dead white orchid he'd passed on to me. "You've got a way with plants, I see."

"Don't start with me," I said.

He pulled up a chair, lightly clapped his hands, and placed one on each knee.

Somewhat distracted, he said, "So, are we cool with what happened last night?"

Wow. He got right to it. I was as much impressed as I was annoyed that he'd chosen to bring it up so quickly.

"Yeah, it's okay. No big deal," I said.

About to start another sentence he paused and looked at me sort of funny.

"What?" I asked. Hoping that a poppy seed from my peanut-butter-and-jelly-bagel breakfast had not elected to hang out between my teeth. Or maybe it was the orchid, giving me the finger behind my back.

Struggling, he said, "It's just that . . . I don't know how to say this . . ."

Oh my . . . where was he going?

"You've got this dark 'gook' at the tip of your nose."

He let out this short and very guylike laugh and I just sat there paralyzed, trying to figure out what it could possibly be. Also hoping that if I blinked a few times I could wish him right out of my office and grab the small mirror from my makeup bag.

"Please tell me you're joking . . ."

Still smiling, he answered, "Uh, no, sorry, I'm not."

"Hang on a second." I looked left into my reflection on my computer screen. Horrified, I tried to smudge it off, but it was stuck. What the??!

"Viv. Take it easy. I think it's the wax from that candle."

I put my pointer finger on the spot in question, and moved it around a bit, and indeed, he was correct. Pretty!

"I'll be right back," I said and, with my hand over my nose, ran to the bathroom. I scrubbed the ashy dark wax off with warm water and returned looking like Rudolph the Red-Nosed Reindeer.

"Okay, where were we?"

"Nowhere really. I wanted to just make sure that you got home okay and I wanted to see if you were going to be there tonight. Don't make yourself crazy worrying and miss it."

"What makes you think I'd do something like that?" I said with a smirk.

He got up from his chair. "Hum. Let's just say, I'm on to you." Then he left.

With one foot out the door I shouted, "Andrew!" and he turned and I said "Gotcha!"

I spent the next few hours coming up with mock album ideas in my head and then, later, produced a small visual presentation. This new project was just the challenge I needed to get through the day. I came up with six different categories and twelve songs for each. I searched our archive for photos for covers that could work back to the themes of each record. This would have normally been a project that I'd work on with Drew, but I wasn't up for it. Guesstimating that the "kiss factor" would disseminate in a few days and then I'd bring him up to speed. In the meantime I phoned May and invited her to develop the concept with me. She was thrilled to oblige and asked Marni to pick up the rest of her pizza-party duties.

We chose music from different eras, 1960 to present. Instead of worrying about the details, what songs were actually "getable," we focused on what songs would be fun. After lunch May and I spent the rest of the afternoon on market research and consumer spending habits when it came to music, specifically female spending habits. Then of course, who or what our competition was, if any, and the ideal ways in which to roll it out. I've definitely learned never to present a creative idea without numbers and stats to back it up.

The project was bittersweet for May. She and I both knew that this was the stuff she should be doing full time. Not collating documents and coordinating conference rooms, but I reminded her that things would go her way in good time. And really, who of us hasn't paid our dues???

"Have you called your family, or Jack, or Sophie to tell them to tune in tonight?" she said as we started cleaning up. She gave me this look as though she knew I hadn't. Sort of a *shame-on-you* type thing.

"I've been really busy today May, so no, I haven't yet."

"Viv, if you don't, I will."

"I'll get a tape or something okay? And besides, my parents don't have cable."

"Vivian . . ." She handed me my telephone.

"All right!"

I got Jack first. By this time I had talked him into getting a cell phone. He still hadn't mastered it, but no one really besides me ever called it, so you know. Anyway, he was floored and just a few streets away from my office. (For some reason this didn't seem odd to me at the time.) "I'll come upstairs and watch it with you guys," he suggested.

I covered up the phone and whispered to May, "He wants to watch it here???"

She nodded her head and waved her hand about, urging me to say okay.

So I did.

Sophie was on Long Island but I managed to reach her. Although she was still up to her eyeballs in work, she vowed to find a TV somewhere and watch it. I phoned my brother, Joseph, who at first was furious that I'd given him all of thirty minutes' notice. He hung up on me soon after, which indicated to me that he had every intention of figuring something out. Last were my folks, who first argued back and forth about whose idea it was not to have cable and then threw out a bunch of neighbors to call to watch the show with and/or tape it.

At just ten of seven I was finished. I had done the right thing, according to May's ethical standards anyway. Somehow it was just making me more uptight. In the next instant, Marni came to get us, letting me know that everyone had already starting making themselves comfortable and that Sheryl had just opened a fancy bottle of wine.

"You coming?" May asked when she saw that I all but ignored Marni's reminder.

"You go. I'll be there in a second."

"I'll be back here to get you just in case you decide to flake, you know."

"I know," I said.

As May left, I leaned against the window at the back of my office. It was cold or I was nervous or both so I wrapped my arms around my chest, sort of like a virtual hug. I was as thrilled as I was petrified. I thought about the girl I was before I left school, the one who only saw this kind of shit in the movies. Surreal. The journey thus far was an incredible one, and I only hoped I had what it took to endure it. I twisted my hair up into my customary mess of a knot, grabbed an Altoid from my desk drawer, glanced quickly at the photo of my parents, housed in a small silver frame I'd gotten as a wedding favor some months before. This moment was as much theirs as it was mine. Good for them, I thought, having never given me their blessing. Stubborn as I am, the odds were that I might have never tried to make it this far if they'd ever thought I could/should.

Whether this interview was just the beginning of many or in the event that it would be my first and last, at the very least it existed. And that, in and of itself, at least for me, was triumphant.

Long story short, I would have much preferred to sit Indian style in profile in front of a bad mirror under harsh lights, naked, eating bonbons, than to have had to watch myself on television. But . . .

twenty-five

Sheryl wasn't the only one who'd decided that alcohol would be needed to get through that evening. Drew had brought a bottle of wine and ordered a case of champagne. And funny, too, it wasn't as if anyone thought to wait to break it all out at the conclusion of my segment for a celebratory toast. Nope. My colleagues had gone through three bottles before it even started. That says a lot, don't you think?

When the interview ended everyone cheered and clapped wildly. Hugging me, laughing, making references to my answers, remarks, and reactions. Everyone was pretty happy. Including the witches of work-wick who gave me three petite grins and simultaneous thumbs-ups. Stan did end up toasting me and I followed by toasting Sheryl.

Jack, who had arrived while I was procrastinating in my office and was in the conference room already waiting for me, grabbed my hand and squeezed it tight once it was over. "I'm so proud of you, Vivian." Then he gave me a tender kiss on the check and a giant bear hug that nearly made me go down a cup size or two.

Out of the corner of my eye, I saw Drew across the room. He raised his glass to me and mouthed, *Congratulations*.

I smiled and mouthed, *Thank you*.

I thought we'd all end up at Luvas that night but May insisted I go home and veg out. "Get her out of here already!" was actually how she phrased it to Jack.

"No no, we'll stay and help you clean up," I said.

"Thanks but it's okay," she said. "Why start now?"

"Ouch!" I said, cracking up.

"Not tonight, Viv. This is your night, I'm not going to let you spend it here," she insisted.

I was about to excuse myself and head back over to my office to grab my stuff but Marni had already done it for me. "Here," she said, passing on my bag and jacket. "We'll see you tomorrow."

"Aw, thanks Marn," I said. "Thank you."

She smiled and with May walked us to the elevator.

"So what do you feel like doing?" I asked Jack once we were out on the street.

"Hmmm. I don't know. You hungry?" he asked.

"Aren't I always?" I answered.

"You wanna order in?"

"Definitely," I said. "But can we hang at my place? I need to walk Omelet."

"Sure," he said.

We decided to take a train downtown. It was quicker and I was famished. Back on street level my voice mail went off wildly. My parents had called, my brother had called, Sophie, my mom's friend Vera, Jack's sister. Every message was filled with so much energy; everyone freaking out over what they had just seen. That made me feel good.

"So what did you think?" I asked Jack. ". . . be honest."

"What did I think? I think it was fucking brilliant. You were great and you looked beautiful."

"Please," I argued. "I looked like a transvestite with all that makeup. And how about my tapping foot? Very professional."

"You're nuts," he said. "And I'm not even going to try to argue with you 'cause I know you'll never believe it for yourself so . . ."

"Okay, so anyway . . . what else is going on, huh?"

"Let's see," he said. "Not too much. Lisa actually made a suggestion the other day that I thought was pretty interesting."

"Oh yeah," I said. "About what?"

"You know that end table I made for Tom? For his birthday last year?"

"Yeah."

"Well, she thinks I should make some more stuff. And try to sell it in this fancy furniture shop in Soho. She takes yoga or something like that with the owner of the place and thinks he'd like my stuff."

"Oh my God, Jack—you should so totally do that. What a great idea!" I said tugging at his jacket sleeve and hopping up and down like a giddy kid who wants some attention. "Lisa knows what she's talking about, Jack. What an opportunity!"

"Yeah, I think so, too."

"So what's next?" I said. "What's the next thing to do, you know, to get started?"

"Next, we need to wind down and focus on what we just saw on television. I'm not going to let you pretend that it wasn't a big deal."

"You're not?" I said.

"No and that's the problem with you, Viv. You let these special moments in your life pass you by. All of 'em, big ones and small ones, all the time. I don't know why you do that. Being excited for yourself and something you achieve doesn't make you arrogant, you know. Seriously. One day you'll be old and gray and you're gonna look back at all this and realize that you downplayed your whole existence."

"Oh really?" I teased, standing on my tippy-toes grabbing the collar of his jacket, trying to give him a peck or two. Doing it, I guess, to lighten the mood and get off the subject.

We arrived at my apartment and I was never so happy to be home. Jack used his key to unlock my door. He pushed it open with his right hand and tilted his body, suggesting that I should enter first. He smiled at me as I smiled at him, acknowledging this rare but sweet little chivalry thing he was working.

As usual, Omelet basically attacked me when I got in the door. Before I could turn on a light or put down my things or anything.

Finally settled, I grabbed a few menus from my junk drawer in the kitchen, spreading them in my hand like a deck of cards, signaling that I wanted Jack to choose one. He grabbed the white-red-and-green Vito's one. I was psyched. I'd secretly hoped for that one. Too nervous to eat the pizza at the office, I was way in the mood now for Italian. Maybe a creamy cream sauce of one kind or another. And truth be told, had he chosen the Greek, Thai, or Chinese one I would have shuffled them up and asked him to pick again.

"Did you leave that light on again?" he asked gesturing toward my bedroom.

The door was closed but from where we were standing, you

could see light coming from the narrow space between the floor and the door.

I could hear my father's voice, *Do you think I work for Con Edison?* "Shit. I guess I did. . . . One minute." So I walked down the short hall and opened the door, about to switch off the lights.

In one fell swoop I saw my life flash before my eyes.

Ba-bump-ba-bump-ba-bump-ba-bump-ba-bump . . . my heart was about to break through my chest.

I remember clutching the purplish crystal doorknob, never letting it go. My body had frozen up while my bulging eyeballs canvassed my bedroom.

Every bit of furniture was covered in white linen sheets. Ivory vanilla-scented candles were propped up against every corner of the room, my end table, my vanity, and my dresser. Bundles of hybrid cream-and-pink roses adorned the sills of my two windows. And, there were a dozen HUGE black-and-white photos of Jack and me hanging from thick spirally ivory yarn from the ceiling. All at different lengths. A chunky hybrid pink-and-cream rose sat atop and center of each photo, dangling confidently, beautifully.

From beginning to end . . .

Jack and me at a New Year's party
Jack and me and Omelet at Central Park
Jack and me on the beach in Miami
Jack and me at his cousin's wedding
Jack and me at the launch party for the Web site
Jack and me wasting film on the street outside the photo place
Jack and me waiting on Dennis as he finished the New York City Marathon

Jack and me at the base of the mountain snowboarding

Jack and me before/after that Dave Matthews concert

Jack and me at my parents' place

Jack kissing me on the cheek

Jack in a tuxedo, Omelet alongside him in the hall in my

apartment . . .

Finally I let go of the doorknob and walked toward my window. I swear to you, I was wishing that it were open so that I could jump out, for real this time.

"Vivian."

I slowly turned around and saw Jack, in that tux, with Omelet right by his side. (Just like that last picture.)

I put both hands over my mouth, involuntarily shaking my head from side to side. Not wanting this to be real. Loving Jack so much it hurt and knowing that I was about to hurt him, too. Hoping that he'd pick up on that somehow, in some way, and not go through with it. I wanted to say something, I should have said something, but I had no words. I couldn't speak. This was so real. So enormous. Everything was so beautiful. More beautiful than I'd ever thought something in real life could actually be. He didn't love me, I thought. He loved the idea of me. But I wasn't me. I wasn't me. I wasn't me.

He motioned for Omelet to walk toward me, which he did and he then said, "Okay Omelet, now sit boy, sit boy."

Dutiful, Omelet plunked down and sat there staring at me. Jack walked toward me. He looked so handsome. I'd never seen him in a tuxedo before. He looked like a long-lost member of the Rat Pack. He was lovely.

"This is the part where I need you to notice his collar, Vivian," he said.

But I couldn't move. I was a Popsicle.

"Viv?"

Moving my tepee'd hands from my face to my chin, I said, "I can't."

"It's okay," he said sweetly and knelt down and felt around the bottom of Omelet's neck for his collar. A thick velvet string in a dusty pink color hung from the loop of Omelet's pet tags. At the end was a glimmering ring.

Jack untied it and stayed on his knee . . . he reached up and grabbed my hand away from my face and held it. His hand was trembling, a little bit, and he'd never looked so happy or so innocent.

"I love you, Vivian. You are everything to me. You are the most wonderful woman I've ever met and I want to be with you forever . . ."

Tears were gushing from my eyes. I could feel them meet my lips, fall over and off them. The salt on my mouth.

"Jack," I murmured.

"Shhh . . . I'm almost done," he said as he wiped the sweat from his forehead, smiling at me all the while. "Okay. This is the thing. I know who you are, Vivian. I know who you are. I know why you run. I know how you love. You are the most complex creature and I love all that about you . . . so let me be with you. Let me take care of you. I will always love you and I will always take care of you."

Fighting back more tears, pushing for more words, I could only find, "Jack."

"Vivian . . ." he began. "Vivian Rose . . . will you marry me?"

twenty-six

would have loved to have said yes. Have had the good fortune of being certain. But timing is everything I guess. Looking back, could Jack have been the one for me? Maybe. Was I at risk of losing him? Definitely. But in that moment, a blushing bride-to-be I was not.

As I stared down into his big bright eyes, knowing that my answer was going to crush him, I just couldn't say no. I didn't have the heart. I timed out, I guess. Wanting to take what could have been the last long look I'd have left. His image brought with it a huge sense of hope and love and togetherness. Safety above all else. And I just couldn't go there with him. Not yet. Not now.

Minutes felt like hours and after a short moment, I think Jack knew that it wasn't going to happen. And rather than ask again, or make it easy on me by saying something, anything, he decided to keep waiting for my response. Maybe he, too, was hoping this all wasn't real. That this wasn't happening to him. And slowly, his gaze of delight turned into one of anger. He got up off his knee and held the ring within the palm of his hand. Shaking it a bit, like you would dice or something. With his other hand, he loosened the cream-colored satin tie from his neck and still refused to look elsewhere, other than at the coward he was in love with.

Omelet broke the silence, picking up on the intensity; he put his cold nose on my hand, pushing me to pet him.

"So that's it then. You aren't even going to say anything? Are you really this cruel?" His chin quivered as he spoke.

Tears still rolling down my face, all I could verbalize was, "I'm sorry."

He looked down and shook his head. He sighed in disgust. "You're going to let this be another moment then, huh, Viv?" He looked up, the tone and sound of his voice revving like a fueled engine . . . "You're going to let this be another FUCKING MOMENT!"

I winced at the force of his voice, the fire in his face. I had never heard him scream before. It shook me to my bones. He seemed to take pleasure in my reaction if for no other reason than to see me react to something.

He sat at the foot of my bed. His head in his hands. He placed the ring beside him and allowed Omelet to console him.

"That's it, Vivian. I'm out. I can't take this anymore."

Still, I said nothing.

"You're like a corpse, you know that? You don't allow yourself to FEEEEEEEEEL anything. Once it gets too good you tune out."

He went on. "I can't live my life like this. I can't." I heard him sniffle and as he looked at me, a lone tear dripped from the corner of his eye. It looked painful. He looked like he was in agony, and as much as I wanted to console him, kiss him, make love to him, say yes to him, it was as if an invisible glass wall had barricaded me off. I couldn't break through it, climb over it or underneath it, to save him from me. I just stood there. Hating myself for the both of us.

He stood up and walked out, scratching the back of his head with one hand, holding his necktie with another. His silhouette got fuzzier and fuzzier as he walked through my apartment and out my door. He didn't even bother to shut it. I could hear it creaking slowly as its own weight ultimately did it for him.

Omelet found the spot on my bed where Jack had sat and circled it, finally lying right there. He looked at me inquisitively. His ears straight up, he cocked his head from side to side before he rested it on the bed. He thought I'd made a big mistake. I knew it.

I scolded myself for not having made a point of talking to Jack that first second I'd seen him when I'd gotten back from my parents' house. This would never have happened had I not been so selfish. I was waiting for the best time for me, when I was most comfortable to talk.

How dare I? Jack had never been anything but loving and kind and amazing. Always. Always. Always. *Wake up, Vivian!* I shouted silently. *Wake the fuck up!!!*

When things got bad, I'd forgotten how to feel bad. When things were great, I'd lost that sensation, too. A long time ago. Jack was right and I guess he thought proposing would somehow wake me up. It would be the cold shower I'd need to be the woman he thought I was. But it didn't work. It backfired. His proposal only removed me from the situation. I can't really explain it. It was outer-bodily. I experienced what had just happened from the sidelines. Now I couldn't even allow myself to cry. My tears were only obstinate remnants of emotions I could barely feel.

Sitting beside Omelet, staring out onto the beautiful sanctuary that Jack had created in my bedroom, looking at these images, images that were so full of meaning, so vibrant, I wondered why it was that I had not even considered the idea of saying, *Yes, I'll marry you, just not now.* At the playground that night, back home, when I came to the conclusion of career-before-marriage—if that were really true and really what I wanted, then, I wondered, why was an engagement so far-fetched? It could be months and years before I'd have to walk down the aisle. Jack and I could determine all that later, couldn't we?

It dawned on me, too, that had any of these photos been a piece of the puzzle that was the wallpaper of Luvas, they'd fit in perfectly. Anyone could look at them, at us, and think that the two people in them were happy together.

I was consumed with confusion. Do people get engaged if only to put off marriage? No, that didn't sound right. But if I knew that I loved Jack, and I knew that I did, and he was good to me, why would I want to spend my life without him? Or with anyone else? I didn't, did I?

I looked at the ring, beautiful, just sitting there, instigating further thought.

If there were anything I'd want to do for Jack, it would be to make him happy. Give him me, I guess, if that's what he wanted. Suddenly I felt wicked, though. Thinking that perhaps I'd said no just to push him away. Maybe I didn't want him to love me. Not like this. The real way. I wanted him to love hanging out with me. Love being with me. But love me, no.

It was as if I'd been poisoned or something. As if I'd annihilated my insides and in so doing, become half a person. Half a woman. I could only offer what was on the outside. Do you know what I mean? Mark had done his damage, but he wasn't the only one to blame. I'd abused myself, too. Taking it all those years, and instead of running, I'd learned to exist like THIS. Like this! It was pathetic. Pathetic. Utterly detached. And every time I wanted to ask for help, I just couldn't. I still can't.

What would I say? I am the embodiment of an ad campaign for God's sake . . . Just do it! Yeah, that's me. How can the girl who's supposed to be bold and brave, be weak and lost? That was my "thing"; I'd made a living as the underdog. The relatable virtual best bud who was great at giving advice but when it came to matters of my own heart, well, that was my little secret.

My personal relationships were consistently at a standstill. And I had the advantage because in a fast-paced world where all of us have our own sets of problems and pressures, delusions and expectations, we all believe what we want to believe. Taking a better look at those things and people closest to us can get dangerous, because then the world as we know it, the way we like to believe that it is, the world that works for us, becomes more complicated. And who consciously looks for trouble anyway?

It wasn't as though I had resentment toward my friends and family 'cause they didn't choose to figure me out; not at all. I was just real good at packaging myself. So good, in fact, that I'd often fool myself from time to time. Case in point: tonight. What a fucking disaster. Up until now, Jack and I had gotten on just fine. He never dared to broach the "Mark" topic with me, assuming, of course, that I'd gotten past it like most women do. (Do they really?) And why should he? Everything was always "fine." Well, maybe now he was having second thoughts.

My obsession to fix what was broken needed a revision, I thought. I'd been getting by with Krazy Glue till now. Fixing a broken chair means replacing the leg with a new one. Permanent. And if that doesn't work, then you get a new chair. Gluing it all back together is simply a repair. Temporary.

Would accepting Jack's proposal be the right step for me? Bold and brave, that's me, right? Keep pushing forward, blah, blah, blah. Or would it be a signature Krazy Glue move that would only throw me farther into the abyss? Was letting him go the only way I'd wake up? When I realized I'd lost him?

I decided to try on the ring. Don't ask me why. I just somehow thought the decision might be a little less mysterious and vague if, by some chance, I donned it with excitement. Maybe being engaged would be fun? Planning a wedding, registering . . . I've heard that's a blast. Maybe I would like being part of another, half of a whole. And the scary element would disappear.

I picked it up and wasn't sure which hand it was meant to go on. I knew which finger, but hand, I wasn't sure. I'm a righty so I went left, thinking it might be difficult to type and write wearing a ring. (I'm not a big jewelry person, I should tell you, so this really was all very Greek to me.)

I slid it down my finger. It was a little snug, but after a good push it was on. It was so girly, I thought. *Oh, look at me, I'm so girly*. I stretched out my arm and, with my hand upright, took a nice long look at it. I looked over to Omelet to see what he thought. He wasn't all that interested. He raised his head a bit but then let it fall back onto the mattress. He added a "ho-hum" for sound effect. God, would my dog leave me, too?

I had the ring on for less than five minutes before I simply had to take it off. It was really tight. Felt like it was gnawing at my skin. With three fingers of my right hand I pulled it off. Or rather, tried to take it off. But it wasn't budging. No worries, I just needed to stand up, I guessed. I had more strength and balance standing upright than I did slouched over my bed.

So I stood up and tried again. No dice. I started to panic. The more I tugged, the worse it felt. The worse it felt, the more nervous I'd get. The more nervous I got, the more I'd sweat. The more I'd sweat, the higher my blood pressure got. The higher my blood pressure got, the more I'd sweat, the more nervous I'd get, the more it would hurt, the harder I'd try, and the faster my finger would swell up to look more like my thigh!!!

Oh my!

Oh my, oh my, oh my!

Then, from my bedroom, I heard noises, voices coming from my hallway. Then a doorbell, then a "Hello! Anybody in here?" and a, "Shhh, we could be 'disturbing them,' " hee hee hee ha ha ha.

"Jack! Viv!" That was Sophie's voice!

I walked toward the door, slowly. Confused, embarrassed . . . by this time my face was swollen, red; I had sweat so much that I looked like I had sideburns what with the random strands of hair, soaked, sticking to each cheek. I kept my left hand behind me, wiped my nose off, and came to the door.

There, huddled in my hallway, were: Sophie, May, my brother Joseph, Lisa, Tom, Jack's sister Gina, Dennis, and Matt. Each with his or her own accessory—balloons, flowers, champagne, stuffed animals. I thought I would be sick. They saw me and immediately reversed their smiles.

Sophie pushed my brother and Lisa aside and grabbed my shoulders. "Oh my God, Vivian, are you okay?"

"No. No I'm not," I said and took my hand from behind my back and showed her the first of my many problems.

Just then, a chorus of apprehensive laughter came from the peanut gallery that was our friends.

"The ring's stuck . . ." Gina said. "The ring's just stuck. Jack must be out getting some . . . I don't know, gel, or jelly or something."

"Of course . . ." sighed Tom.

"Of course," laughed Joseph.

Sophie sank down a bit in order to get a better view of my eyes and whispered, "Is that it, Viv? It's just stuck, that's all? Everything else is okay?"

I broke down. I started crying and mumbled, "No, that's not it. It, it, it was a big disaster. Jack's gone. The ring is stuck."

"What did you say to him? Did you say *no*, Viv?" she said.

"No . . ."

"So you said yes then?"

"No . . ."

May brought me over to the sofa, Lisa got me a glass of water, and Gina stared me down, as any big sister would if in fact a girl had said no to her brother's proposal. The boys, of course, were conferencing in the kitchen, not knowing what the hell to say or do.

"Tom . . . get us a lubricant of some kind, would you?" Lisa shouted.

"A what?" Tom asked.

"A lubricant, Tom. Something slippery, gelly . . ."

"What happened Vivian?" Sophie asked.

"I can't talk about it now, Soph. My finger is killing me and I think I'm going to faint." I was seasick sans the sea.

"Okay, okay," she said, holding my other hand and rubbing my arm. "We don't have to talk about it right now. We don't have to. Where's Jack, honey?"

"I don't know. I don't know."

They realized it would only make matters worse if I spoke. 'Cause each time I did, I just got myself more upset.

Tom and Matt carried over a cluster of products and we tried everything, from mayo to conditioner, butter to baby oil, nothing. It was just making it worse and worse.

"Somebody needs to call Jack. . . . I mean really," Gina said. Everyone looked her way but me. I was afraid to. "What?" she said defensively. "He can get in touch with the jeweler, and maybe he can do something."

Sophie interrupted and confessed, "The ring came from my mother's jeweler in Pennsylvania, Gina." She looked at me with this *Oh well, I'm sorry but I had a hand in this* look. "I don't think there's much he can do for us or tell us that we don't know or haven't tried already, you guys."

May asked me if I'd be okay with going to the emergency room and I nodded. She took control of the situation and looked at Sophie like, *This is getting too weird. Let's get the fuck out of here.*

Sophie got my coat and May told everyone that we were going to go to St. Vincent's Hospital, the emergency room. Joseph said he'd stick around, keep an eye out for Omelet. And I don't really remember what anybody else said, who stayed or left or whatever. I was pretty out of it by then.

Clutching their champagne, but letting their CONGRATULATIONS! Mylar balloons float up up and away into the sky, we three got into the first cab we saw and headed straight uptown.

"I think we should open this," Sophie said.

"Good call," May agreed.

To give you an idea of how bad it was, I couldn't hold the bottle up myself. My left hand was useless and beyond sensitive to touch. So the girls held my "baby bottle," if you will, and I drank and drank and drank. Didn't really swallow much, instead it dribbled down and all over my (white) blouse.

"Everything's going to be fine, Viv, I promise," Sophie said. "Everything's going to be fine."

I didn't say much of anything on the ride to the hospital. Instead I stuck my head out the window like a dog and prayed that I wouldn't get sick.

We finally got there and soon realized that our ring crisis was not that high on the ER's priority list. I was assured that although it hurt, my finger wouldn't fall off, and I was given an anti-inflammatory I think and some Tylenol to tide me over. A second nurse came over with some paperwork for me to fill out and an ice pack to try to reduce the swelling.

Together we each snuck swigs of the champagne 'cause we knew it was going to be a very long night.

twenty-seven

One hour followed the next, and the hospital staff politely pacified each of us again and again. The pain hadn't subsided but at least it had become familiar. Nearing midnight and having calmed a ways down, I gave an edited version of the evening's mishaps to my friends. I, too, got some information of my own, such as how this had all happened, who knew what, who did what, and so on and so on. As the story unfolded, I felt worse and worse. I wanted to know but I didn't.

Jack had designed the ring himself and had it "approved" by Sophie; then together they'd driven down to Pennsylvania and in one weekend had the setting done and my father's permission one, two, three. He had used the stone from his grandmother's ring, Sophie had helped decorate my room, May had the photos converted to black and white and enlarged, and we'd all had a dinner reservation for ten at Babbo.

Who knew? Not too many people at first. My family, his family, Sophie's of course. May, and a handful of Jack's friends. Stan had overheard Sophie and May on the phone a few days prior and then evidently, when Jack came up to the office to watch the interview, Stan congratulated him in front of everyone and that got people talking and then, May admitted, when we left, everyone pretty much figured it out and well, by that time it was common knowledge.

"Terrific," I said sarcastically.

"I'm so sorry, Vivian," Sophie said in near tears. "Honestly, somehow I thought, I assumed, you'd say yes. I would have never . . ."

"Shhh. It's okay. I understand and I don't blame you."

"Honest?" she said.

"Honest."

"It was actually pretty funny, Vivian, 'cause when you called me to tell me about the rescheduling of the interview thing, I thought you were calling me to tell me . . . well, you know. And then, all I wanted to do was watch the interview with you and well, I couldn't, because you thought I was still out on Long Island . . ."

"Yeah. You both really went through a lot for me. Put a lot of time and romantic energy into it, huh."

They both nodded, very bummed that it all didn't have a happy ending.

May then asked, "So what are you going to do now, V? After tonight, that is?"

"I don't know. I really don't."

Sophie got up to scope out the vending machine scenario. We were all famished.

"For what it's worth, Vivian," May admitted, "I think it takes a pretty brave woman to do what you did."

"It's not about being brave May . . . trust me," I said.

"Look, from where I'm sitting, for whatever the reason or reasons that you weren't ready, you still followed your instincts."

I looked at her in a very *I don't know about that* sort of way.

"You did. It just didn't feel right. Tonight wasn't the night, is all. Most women would say yes because they were just afraid to say something else, and then unveil a bombshell later on. You didn't do that and that's why I respect you so much."

"Thanks . . . I guess."

I leaned over a bit, focused on a spot in the floor, and shook my head from side. With my good hand, I brushed the hair away from my face. I heard May whisper, "Viv, Vivian, Viv." And when I sat up straight and opened my eyes, there was Jack, alongside Sophie, back in a sweatshirt and jeans, bearing fast food and a forced smile.

"Hi?" I said timidly.

"Hey," he said, barely looking at me. "Hey May."

"Hi Jack," May said with preventive sympathy in her voice. "Soph, let's take a walk and give these two some privacy."

"Sure," Sophie said.

"Why don't you guys get going. I can take over from here," he said.

"Yeah?" Sophie said, looking my way for a reaction.

"Sure," I said.

"Okay." They grabbed their things and gave us each a hug and kiss. "Call us in the morning," May said.

"Love you," Sophie said.

I just smiled and watched them walk away.

"How am I supposed to stay mad at you when you go and get yourself in a mess like this?" he said warmly.

I raised my shoulders up and down in an *I-don't-know* manner.

"Big Mac?" he said, grabbing one from the bag.

"Yes, thanks."

I had trouble unraveling the paper it was packaged in. Jack helped out.

"So do you mind if I don't ask how or why this happened?" he said.

"No," I said. "I'd actually prefer it that way."

I wanted to tell him that I loved him. I wanted to tell him how sorry I was. How handsome he'd looked in that tux. I wanted to say something but everything that came to mind sounded like a cheesy cliché, felt inappropriate, or was just way too light.

Finally it was my turn to see the doctor. Jack came with. In normal situations the walk down the hallway would have come with Jack resting his hand at the base of my neck.

This time he lagged behind both the nurse and me. If this was the beginning of the end, I hated it already.

We entered a small space quarantined by long blue curtains rather than walls. I could hear the conversations of many; I could smell the smells of many. I wanted to be anywhere but there.

"So," the nurse said, "what happened here?"

Neither of us said anything at first and then she looked down at my hand and Jack just said, "I proposed," very plain and simply.

The nurse looked my way and with her first real expression of the evening caught my eyes and said, "Oh! Congratulations."

I looked over at Jack and said, "Thanks."

"Okay. This is making much more sense now. The excitement of big events can do strange things to our bodies."

"Evidently," Jack said.

"Well, you'll be happy to know that nine times out of ten we can work the ring off the finger without having to surgically re-move it."

"Surgically remove it?" I asked.

"Yes."

"What's involved in that?" Jack asked.

"Just a very mild anesthesia and a small electrical device that can cut through the platinum."

Before I could even ask what that meant exactly, the doctor arrived.

He said hello to each of us, took a look at my finger, asked how long it had been stuck, reviewed my chart, and disappeared again, promising he'd be back in a few minutes. The nurse followed.

I took one look at Jack and started crying again. I was a nervous wreck.

He remained polite and distant. I couldn't blame him.

Back was the nurse, then the doctor. The nurse consoled me and handed me some tissues. And what followed was another twenty minutes of failed attempts to get the ring off. From a tourniquet-style rope debacle to another mysterious lube job and then a fancy wrench to stretch the band a bit, but nothing worked.

It was decided that we'd get surgical. The nurse would be back, she said, with an anesthesiologist in a moment.

Finally Jack reverted to his old self. Holding my other hand and trying to distract me, talking sports and then about the interview. It was comforting for about a second but it got awkward quickly.

We didn't even make our way home from the hospital until almost three in the morning. Neither of us said much. Jack had driven his car so the ride home was filled with CD selections and uncomfortable silences. Where's a chatty cabdriver when you really need one?

As we turned onto my street he pulled over and put the car in park.

"I don't think I can see you anymore," he said, staring out in front of him rather than around and toward me.

I bit my lip and turned away. I didn't want him to see that I was fighting back emotions. Whatever it was that he wanted to say to me, that he needed to say to me, I needed to hear it. I deserved it, no matter how harsh, and I wanted him to get it all out.

"It's been too long, Vivian. What we have now doesn't work for me anymore. I was ready, you know? I wanted more."

"I understand," I said.

I got the sense that he was waiting for an explanation, but I didn't feel like I could give him one.

"I love you, you know," he said and turned toward me.

"I love you, too," I said and reached for his hand but for the very first time, he pulled it away from me and said, "Don't" and that killed me.

"And I feel bad ya know. I feel real bad because I know this is not about me. It's about you. All of this. You're too afraid to let yourself be happy. It's sick."

Okay, that hurt.

"And I feel bad because I wonder if you ever really will feel the way you deserve to feel. I really do. Adored, protected, treasured. All those things." He sniffled a bit and put his hands through his hair and then continued. "You're gonna be very successful, Vivian. I can tell you that for sure. You'll have a great job and accomplish all sorts of things. But you're too sensitive a person to be on your own. Success ain't gonna do it all for you. And what's killing me is that I know for sure I'm the guy for you, and when you finally figure that out, if you finally figure that out, well, I'll be long gone."

Okay. I think that about did it. I'd taken all the "honest" remarks I could tolerate. "I don't know what to say, Jack. I think we need some time . . ."

He cut me off. "*No. We don't need any time. It's over. I can't even look at you. I just feel pity and hate. It's done. It's over.*"

"I'm sorry Jack . . . I just can't make that kind of commitment right now."

He shook his head from side to side, looked out his window, and said, "God, you were a huge waste of my time."

"That's it then?" I whimpered.

"Yes."

Me and my bandaged hand got out of his car. I was a huff and a puff from getting nasty, from saying something that would hurt him or that I'd regret, if I stayed there for one more minute. It wasn't as though I thought I had the right to, it was just the only thing I knew how to do.

I walked down my block and into my building, having never looked back. By the time I got home Joseph was asleep on my couch and the apartment looked like a tornado had hit it. My bedroom still looked like heaven and I still felt like hell. I removed the linen sheets and found a safe spot in my bed. I didn't bother setting my alarm, or checking my messages, or brushing my teeth, or anything. I curled up nice and snug and lay there in the dark, faceup, wondering if I had made the worst decision of my life and preparing myself for my parents and everything else that would come along with the very public knowledge of a fairy tale gone awry.

twenty-eight

Each time I felt sorry for myself that next day and those that followed, I would just as quickly think of Jack and what he must have been going through. Sure, it sucked to be me, but I was on the giving end. He'd been rejected in the worst way I could imagine and that helped me to put my shit into perspective right away.

Sure, my cover was blown, but in a strange subtle way it was a relief. I no longer carried the weight of a relationship on my shoulders. Trying always to convince myself to be grateful, content, and complete . . . the confused recipient of a seemingly charmed life. It felt good to be real. I was as much of a mess as the next person. And now the cat was out of the bag.

Having not been able to sleep much, I woke up relatively early and got to work before the cavalcades rolled in. My office was just as I'd left it and not a single message was on my answering machine. I thought it best to call my parents and get it over with while I still had my privacy.

The dial tone was unusually loud and deep. It rang once, twice, and on the third ring my father answered.

"Hello," he said.

"Hi Dad. It's me."

"Yes?" he said.

His response of choice was marginal. Aggravated, disinterested, angry? Was I reading too much into it? Maybe.

"Well, I just thought you and Mom should know that . . ."

"We know," he said coldly. "Your brother phoned us last night." His phrases lacked emotion, which could only mean that he was very disappointed in me. My dad doesn't know how to fly off the handle; that's my mom's gig.

"I . . ." I didn't know how to respond to him.

"It's a shame. Jack is a wonderful young man, a real stand-up guy that both your mother and I would have liked to welcome into our family."

"Yes," I said. "I know."

"I'm not too sure you do. (Pause) Here's your mother."

Great. Here we go.

"Vivian. Vivian dear. It's Mom."

"Hi."

"Listen Vivi, everyone gets cold feet. It's very understandable. I'm sure if you give Jack a call, he'll find it in his heart to forgive you."

Were my parents living in the Dark Ages???

"Mom. You don't seem to get it. If I wanted to marry Jack then I would have said yes last night."

Her voice changed instantly. "So then what is it, Vivian? Tell me that, will you? What is it that you want?"

"Ma . . ." I was about to give up. She just didn't get it and it was useless to try to make her understand.

"You're very fancy now, I know," she said sarcastically. "But do you think you're going to meet a second man who wants to marry you? Or maybe a third and fourth? Life does not work that way, Vivian, and you may be too young to understand that right now but I'm not. I want you to get your head back on straight and do what's best. Do what's right."

"Or what, Mom. Or what? Are you going to make Joseph an only child and outcast me, too?"

"How dare you?" she huffed, nearly blowing a gasket. But this was my moment to get things where they needed to be. To set boundaries. This was a moment that needed to be seized.

"How dare you, Mom? How dare you pressure me into doing something I'm not ready to do just because you and Dad want it to be so. Get over it! I'm not yours to control. You can love me if you want to and care about me, but control me—no way."

Shocker: She hung up the phone.

Wonderful.

I gave myself an A for effort and decided that this was a big bacon-egg-and-cheese moment, so I dialed the deli downstairs and had one, sorry two, delivered.

I slowly and deeply inhaled and exhaled, over and over, to try to calm down. There would be no tears today.

I phoned the pharmacy and asked when my prescription would be ready (antibiotic and painkiller) and thought about asking if they recommended anything for guilt.

Sheryl knocked briefly on my door, a bunch of lilies in hand and halfway through "Congra—" She did a double take when she saw my bandaged hand and wounded expression and then she finished, "—tulations."

"Not exactly," I admitted.

"God. I'm sorry, Vivian," she said sincerely. "Maybe these will cheer you up?" She handed me the flowers. "They were meant to be, well . . . just take them."

"Thanks," I said.

"You want to tell me about it?"

"Not really. Not now," I said.

"No worries. It's okay. I understand. I'm just next door if you need me."

"Sure," I said. "Thanks, Sheryl."

"I'll just close this . . ." she said as she left.

"Thanks."

I flipped on my computer and started a Word document that read, "I said no so don't bother . . ." I thought I'd print it out and tape it outside my office and save everyone the discomfort.

I deleted it.

Sophie and I exchanged instant messages. She would meet me at my place at nine P.M. jammies in tow, and would be bringing the usual:

- Movies: *Mystic Pizza, About Last Night, Working Girl, Baby Boom,* and *Good Will Hunting*
- Bioré nose strips
- Profiteroles, vanilla ice cream, and chocolate syrup

The rest of the day was filled with explanations and awkward silences. But as the sun began setting late in the afternoon, everyone was more than well informed and it was back to business as usual.

Now was as good a time as any to meet with Drew and hand over the work that May and I had done. Maybe see what he thought, if he wanted to revise it at all, add a few things. We met in his office, we called May in, and we went through it point by point. He dug it. I mean he really, really dug it.

"Sometimes the simplest ideas are the best ideas," he said, still marveling at our outline.

"Amen," May said.

He was impressed and enthusiastic about pitching it to Stan and Hawk. He asked May to get a meeting scheduled for early the following week; in the meantime, he said, he and his team would take what we'd done visually (which currently looked like an arts-n-crafts project) and turn it into something techie and cool.

I couldn't help but notice the photo that Drew had of "But" on his desk. It got my attention in a way that I still don't fully understand. She was thin, which pissed me off. She was sophisticated, which made me jealous. And she looked uncomfortable; difficult to please, which made me skeptical.

"Okay then. This all sounds great," I said and walked out. May lingered and I just went along my way. Being around Drew felt strange. Being around myself felt strange. As happy as I was that he was excited about the music project, I had to keep moving. Keep busy. And as much as I knew that Drew had nothing to do with what happened with Jack, somewhere in the back of my brain, that kiss lingered.

When I got back I saw an e-mail from Sheryl—she had cc'd Stan—letting me know that the feedback from the interview was coming in and it was all very positive. That was good news.

In the midst of my reply to Sheryl, Lisa had called, checking up on me. Asking how I was doing.

"I'm doing fine," I said. "How's Jack?"

"He's pretty torn up, Vivian. I'm not going to lie to you," she confided. "Maybe we should meet up after work for a cocktail or something?"

"I'm not really up for it, but thanks. I didn't get much sleep last night and I still need to get over to the pharmacy before it closes tonight. Rain check maybe?"

"Are you sure, Viv?"

"Yeah, I'm fine Lisa, really. You're sweet to be concerned."

"Well, of course I'm concerned," she fired back. "You're my friend and last night was, well, it was pretty messed up."

"Yeah it was, wasn't it. But it will work itself out, right? It has to," I said.

"Maybe tomorrow then?" she said.

"Yeah, maybe tomorrow. Call me tomorrow."

"Okay, sweets, I will. Rest up tonight and please call me if you need me."

When we hung up I felt strange. Lisa was my friend but by association, ya know? It was difficult to imagine us maintaining a relationship without the ties we shared with Jack and Tom. It sucked actually. She was very cool and very smart but what would we talk about? We'd both be cautious about what we said or didn't say. Or maybe I'd want to hang out just to fish for info on Jack? Her, too—info on me, for Tom, for Jack.

Jack was probably my only boyfriend whose friends I really considered to be my own. Mark's, Patrick's, John's—ewwww, no thank you.

This was beginning to feel more like a divorce than a breakup. I wondered how his day was going. If he was missing me or still hating me, even over me, realizing that he could easily find someone a lot more deserving of his affections than myself. In less than twelve hours I had let what had happened demolish what we'd built together. His words in the car had resonated with me; snowed in and trapped with more insecurity and self-doubt, I was beginning to panic, positive that I'd lost my shot.

I was a giant seesaw, back and forth, up and down, all day.

My phone rang again, and I was tempted to let it go straight to voice mail, but my new *Deal with it* mantra had me thinking twice.

"Hello, this is Vivian," I answered.

"Hi Vivian, my name is Victoria Boz. I'm so happy to have gotten you directly."

"Hi Victoria," I said. "What's up?"

"Well, first I must say that your Web site is incredible. My coworkers and I get lost in your journal writing every day . . . during our lunch breaks of course."

Very flattered, I thanked her. "Thanks Victoria. Thank you. I'm so glad you like it."

"Well, that's just it, Vivian. I more than like it. Or shall I say, we more than like it."

"Who's we?" I asked apprehensively.

"I'm an editor, Vivian, at a large publishing company here in New York. After seeing your interview last night, it hit me, your story—your stories, actually—would make for an excellent novel."

This had to be a joke.

"You are kidding me, right?" I said, smiling from ear to ear. My body stiff with anticipation, terror, and absolute delight. Hoping she'd say yes, hoping just as much that she'd say no.

"No. I'm very serious. (I guess she did both.) We love your point of view. You do pen the journal entries yourself, correct?" she asked.

"Yes," I said.

"You tell it like it is, you're funny, you're open. We think women would really enjoy it and, more importantly, relate to you. And besides, we're all sure that there's more to your life than what you give us on a daily basis. The good stuff. That's why a novel, a series of novels perhaps, would be wonderful to produce."

"I'm, I'm, I'm . . . speechless, I guess!"

"Would you be interested in coming in and meeting with a few people here?" she asked.

"Uh, um . . . of course."

"How's tomorrow?" she said.

"Tomorrow?" This was just too unbelievable.

"If you're not busy we'd very much like to meet with you right away."

"Well then, tomorrow it is."

I took down all of her information and tried to remain as cool, calm, and collected as humanly possible until we hung up the phone.

I sat there, paralyzed. Clearly, in the future I'd need to be a lot more careful about what I wished for. It wasn't as though I was being served this opportunity on a silver platter, no work, just luck. Not so. But I knew that this was the culmination of a commitment I'd made to myself long ago.

Be true. Be true. Be true. A struggle that still, as you now know, finds me every single day.

From being cast as the namesake for the Web site, to participating in its development, to being a part of a larger effort making people aware that we even existed—just getting to the likes of Victoria took word of mouth and press coverage. Keeping her interested, visually and emotionally, once she did visit our site was a whole other challenge. Then breaking through my personally spun web of self-consciousness and being honest and forthcoming when I wrote my journal entries every night was now proving to be more than just a vanity assignment. And then of course, the Fashion Television piece. Sheryl working her ass off to secure it . . .

It was all part of a process that was much larger than my own secret wish to write a novel someday. But damn, talk about willing something to happen? Wanting it and then admitting that, being aware of it all the time and working toward it, inch by inch. It had to have factored in somewhere. It had to.

I savored one of my last conversations with Jack. About being proud and happy for an achievement I'd worked hard for. I was applying it even as I thought about it. Feeling like I was on my own for the very first time, without the cradle of my parents or my boyfriend, even if it was just "day one."

I sat there mystified at the way God plays me. She knows my fate but never gives a single inch. She makes me earn it, find it, come hell or high water, all by my lonesome. I knew now that I could not control my destiny, that I could only do my best to get there. The best I could do that day was to feel the joy that was this opportunity. Enjoy it, rather than play it down. Live my reality as I had created it. Day by day.

And who knew if it would actually really happen. How Stan and corporate execs would feel. If Victoria and her peers would even still be interested once they met me face-to-face. And the fact remained: I was a rookie with about a thousand journal entries under my belt. Which, basically, were more of a pastime than a project. No rules. No beginning. No end.

I looked up at the stale commercial cookies-n-cream paneling that was the ceiling. I looked up 'cause I knew she could see me and I let her know that I wanted my life and was accepting her challenge.

"Thanks for the bone," I said.

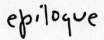

epilogue

Ahhhhhhh, the saga continues, eh?

Yeah, so, *The Autobiography of Vivian: A Novel* came out in June of 2002, and in the velvety words of the late great Mr. Frank Sinatra . . . "I did it myyyyyyy wayyyyyyyyyyy." And obviously, the sequel, *Vivian Lives*, followed suit, and truthfully, the whole thing still gives me goose bumps.

And here I am writing the epilogue, knowing that soon I'll need to start book three in this here trilogy, and it's terrifying, I tell ya . . . 'cause I'm still waiting to see what happens!

The first novel opened a bunch of doors for me; the likes of which I gather will make up book three the way things are looking. And yet again, I find myself conflicted with this "go big or go home" attitude that until recently was just a catchphrase I'd use when doubling down on a pair of aces while blackjacking it in Las Vegas somewhere. And I credit you, the reader, as my instigator of late. Looking to you when the going gets tough and when, actually, the going gets cute if ya know what I mean. ☺

(Stay tuned!) I think my inner voice, the one I described in the beginning of this novel, caught a cheap flight on Jet Blue and is vacationing it somewhere. Ah, so be it.

Allow me to ramble 'cause I've been dying to all the while:

When we think of what we really want out of life, when we allow ourselves to follow our dreams, in all honesty, we go at it alone. Rules never really apply, and Cliff Notes are nonexistent. Really living, rarely looking back, is a high-stakes bet at best, and you've got to get in touch with your inner pit bull and be ready to fight the good fight, be open for a true love, and grab hold of the subtle incongruencies that encapsulate every opportunity. To live the life that dreams are made of, literally, is a destiny in progress. The ultimate challenge. Of which, the details, rest stops, and pitfalls, the practicality of a quest, is ironically never part of the vision. Having started my journey back in 1998, I was too green and too optimistic, too filled with the success stories of a few, to have a single inclination of what I was in for—even best-case scenario. I arrived in New York City ready for anything, prepared for nothing, and my only innate truth was to keep moving.

And, well, it's been a roller-coaster ride ever since—a great one. I didn't realize that all of this would seriously turn my world upside down. Waiting tables at The Figaro, meeting Zack, working at VH1, then the Web site, now the books—I mean c'mon now. It would have been a lot safer to just stay put and reserve the criticisms for someone a lot more sure of who they are and what they stand for. Who would I have been, who could I have been if I hadn't acknowledged my fantasies? I can only leave those questions here on this page.

Living life on its surface, where every decision matters, where every word is etched in stone, every bit of interest could spawn into something beyond the scope of the realistic . . . is as terrifying as it is incredible. I hadn't a clue of the disillusionment, enlightenment, a fierce dedication so mandatory that I'd swear it's morphed into something tangible that follows me around day and night. What it would do to my relationships. How it would edit my life even unbeknownst to me, which has worked out both good and bad in several cases. But no complaints. Honest! I wouldn't and I couldn't have it any other way.

What I do is who I am, and it's a necessity so vital and absolutely my only way down an ever-elusive path of self-discovery. "Two roads diverged in a wooded path and I chose the one less traveled by . . ." yeah, well, obviously. Thanks a lot Robert Frost! It's all a process. ☺

And speaking of paths, a very wise man once said to me (while also quoting singer/songwriter Patti Smith), *Paths that cross, cross again*. And those words comfort me as I reflect, regret, reminisce. As I write, as I think, as I create, and as I try . . . the relationships I've left behind, the experiences I've missed out on, the scenarios that didn't go the way I had wanted them to, I have to believe that, in the end, each will balance the other out and that what was meant to be will be, so long as I am true to myself.

If anything, I hope this novel has given you a laugh or two. Made you smile. Made you think. While not reinventing the wheel, I am definitely sharing my musings for the both of us. For me, a familiar voice feels like an old friend, and who of us can't use another one??? If there is something you want, something you feel—just do it. Quit making excuses, stop thinking you don't have what it takes. Just try. Do it for yourself and do it for all that you come in contact with. A woman on the verge of something big, of something subtle, is a spectacle so magnificent, a feeling so gratifying, a power so palpable, well, for me, it's the only way to live.

That's all I can wish and hope for and that's really the only thing I absolutely know. Don't look to me or to this novel for any-thing else than that. Entertainment with a little somethin' some-thin'. That's all that I'm good for, for now anyway.

Before I write my epilogues I always reread the novel from beginning to end. It actually marks the first and last time I ever read what I write. (I'm too neurotic to look back.) Wite-Out in hand, I kept thinking, God, did I leave a great guy behind? Have I been missing the best years of my life remembering the bad ones? Am I really this insecure? Is my ambition fueled by spite? Was he really worth it? Should I take this part out? Give it a little tweak-a-roo here and there?

I was close, very close, to making this story about someone I wish I was, someone I want to be, rather than the woman I am today. I mean seriously, I was right there. 'Cause I felt so naked and a little too honest at times. That I hadn't done enough or had the enlightenment just yet, to have a story worth telling. But then I thought to myself, yet again, "go big or go home," and I left it all as is. I mean, I've gotten this far on being everything that I am, rather than everything that I'm not—a concept that guides me when playing it safe feels, for the moment, like the better op-tion.

Realizing that with a business on my shoulders and a bunch of books on my back, it does seem fitting that I'm still in the midst of personal and professional upheaval, and it's definitely easier to be nervous about the future when you have no idea what it will bring. (Look, I'd rather fear the unknown than the known.) Maybe I'll fall in love, I mean loooooove. Maybe I'll join the Peace Corps. Maybe I'll bump into a brilliant truth. Maybe I'll fail miserably. But for a thrill-seeking betting woman, letting it ride kinda feels right when you consider the possibilities . . . the end-less possibilities.

If you haven't sensed it already, I'm not all that anxious to truly type "the end" just yet. I so much enjoyed the time I spent writing to you. It's an unabashed connection that we'll have forever, and it's a lot easier for me to feel it, sitting here in the confines of my own space, than out there in the harsh world of expectations, schedules, budgets, bastards, and so on. Penning these books is such a gift that you've given me. Of course, it's therapeutic, that goes without saying, but it's also richly satisfying, like the best brownie you've ever had the pleasure of biting into but then so much better! So, with that, I want to really say "thank you" for spending your free time with me. Not to sound like an airline pilot, but I know that you have a trillion other options when you choose a book to get into, and I am so happy, flattered, and appreciative that you've chosen mine.

Insert Mickey Mouse theme song here: "And now it's time to say good-bye to all our company, M-I-C, see ya real soon, K-E-Y, why? Because we love you! M-O-U-S-E."

Till next time and with all my love,

Vivian

The End.

about the authors

Bronx born, SHERRIE KRANTZ grew up in New York and attended the University of Buffalo. She spent three years as a member of the public relations team at Calvin Klein, Inc., before leaving to become the director of public relations at Donna Karan International. She now lives in New York City with her dogs, Nikki and Stella. In 1999, Sherrie founded Forever After, Inc., parent company to Vivianlives.com, and in 2002, she cowrote *The Autobiography of Vivian: A Novel*. Currently, Sherrie is producing six Vivianlives compilation records for RCA and is developing television and film projects with Paramount and Fox. She and Vivian go way back. ☺

VIVIAN LIVINGSTON is still paying the bills as the digital doyenne of *www.Vivianlives.com*. She's addicted to reality television, still has introspective conversations with her dog, Omelet, and has recently taken up kickboxing, hoping to relieve some virtual tension and kick some virtual ass. She's happily single but on the prowl for Mr. Right, and after cowriting *The Autobiography of Vivian: A Novel*, she's been seen canoodeling with the likes of Eminem, David Beckham, Jimmy Fallon, and Justin Timberlake.

Vivian's story, from the beginning.
Fresh out of college to her bold move to NYC...

As the traditionally traumatic last semester of college winds down, feeling the need for drastic change, Vivian Livingston enters a songwriting contest—and wins. The prize is an incredible weekend getaway to the capital of the universe: New York City.

Yet the moment Vivian and her best friend Sophie set foot in their raw space (AKA their new apartment) in NYC, they know that life in the city is going to be anything but easy. Lacking both dough and direction, Vivian has a rough time with the transition. Even worse, Sophie seems to have found a soul mate—and has left Vivian behind. But Vivian is determined to make her world work, despite a few challenging bumps in the road. Rather than ship out, things begin to shape up, as Vivian not only gets the (virtual) keys to the city, but most important, discovers the keys to her own heart.

Published by Ballantine Books
Available wherever books are sold